I0631381

THE
REAL DEAL

Paritosh Uttam is a software engineer based in Pune. He is the author of the novel _Dreams in Prussian Blue_ (2010), which was later adapted into the award-winning Malayalam film _Artist_. Several of his short stories have appeared in various magazines, newspapers and e-zines. _The Real Deal_ is his second novel.

To know more about him, visit www.paritoshuttam.com

Praise for the author's previous book,
Dreams in Prussian Blue

'Uttam's sense of placement is sharp, with scenes moving like a pictorial storybook, promising the reader of vivid possibilities in the next page.'—The Economic Times

'*Dreams in Prussian Blue* is a reminder of the pleasures of a strong story, briskly told. It's character-driven, written in sober, non-frills prose, and the story keeps you turning the pages at a quick rate.'—Jai Arjun Singh

THE
REAL DEAL

PARITOSH UTTAM

RUPA

For Palash

Published by
Rupa Publications India Pvt. Ltd 2016
7/16, Ansari Road, Daryaganj
New Delhi 110002

Sales centres:
Allahabad Bengaluru Chennai
Hyderabad Jaipur Kathmandu
Kolkata Mumbai

Copyright © Paritosh Uttam 2016

This is a work of fiction. Names, characters, places and incidents are
either the product of the author's imagination or are used fictitiously,
and any resemblance to any actual persons, living or dead,
events or locales is entirely coincidental.

All rights reserved.
No part of this publication may be reproduced, transmitted, or
stored in a retrieval system, in any form or by any means, electronic,
mechanical, photocopying, recording or otherwise, without the prior
permission of the publisher.

ISBN: 978-81-291-3991-7

First impression 2016

10 9 8 7 6 5 4 3 2 1

The moral right of the author has been asserted.

Typeset by Saanvi Graphics, Noida.

This book is sold subject to the condition that it shall not, by way
of trade or otherwise, be lent, resold, hired out, or otherwise
circulated, without the publisher's prior consent, in any form of
binding or cover other than that in which it is published.

PREFACE

Percy was faced with a dilemma that had to be resolved literally by choosing between a red and a blue door, and entering one. Had he been a keener student of history, he might have thought of Paul Tibbets, the pilot of the Enola Gay. Tibbets had had only moments to decide whether to press the button that would abort his mission, or the one that would drop the atomic bomb on Hiroshima. Or, supposing Percy's English was better and he watched English films, he might have thought of Keanu Reeves as Neo in *The Matrix*, asked to choose between a red and a blue pill. But as neither supposition was true, Percy could not fall back on either historical or fictional analogy.

To be fair to him, with only a few moments at his disposal before it became too late, rendering any choice immaterial, he had no time to bother with analogies of any sort. Later, as the enormity of his decision sunk in, he realized that all his pondering and vacillating had been done beforehand. What had happened was simply the logical and natural outcome of all his thoughts, his actions and his character—which made him who he was.

Percy had somehow, though not consciously, known all along that he was destined to face this dilemma. At the last instant, beyond which it would not matter what he decided, Percy moved towards the door he wanted. He had chosen.

CHAPTER 1

Choice was a luxury Percy, aka Paras, sorely missed, ever since he had become conscious of its lack, that is. He obviously had no say about the place of his birth, or where he grew up. But not a day passed when he did not wish that he'd been brought up in a metro like Delhi instead of nondescript Bisalpur, which had absolutely nothing to distinguish it from scores of other towns in western Uttar Pradesh. The man who had had the choice—his father—had fled the hustle-bustle and competition, and resolutely refused to quit the comfort zone of Bisalpur.

But more than anything, Paras bemoaned the injustice of the name thrust upon him at birth. He loathed it. Of the thousands of acceptable Hindu names for boys, his father had to pick Paras Nath in deference to the wishes of his Guruji. Add the surname, and you had Paras Nath Sharma. Its dated 200-year-old feel had not bothered Paras during his childhood. But as he grew out of school and into college, the name made him the butt of ridicule more and more often.

He often cornered his father: 'Why did you give me this name? What was wrong with names like Puneet or even Prakash if it had to start with a "P"?'

His father replied patiently, 'Because Paras is a good name. It means "touchstone".'

'But why the "Nath" after it? It makes me sound sixty years old.'

'You are right,' said his father, fed up. 'The name is too good for you.'

'I agree,' Paras said. 'So I'll take a new name, of which I am worthy, and put it in the papers.'

'Better change your last name also,' his father said.

'It's just Sharma, for God's sake. You make it sound as though it was Ambani.'

After every such exchange, which had become typical and frequent, Paras wished for a choice that nobody else in the whole of mankind had ever had—the privilege of choosing one's parents. He did not remember his father ever being this irritable earlier. He had changed over the last year or two, ever since Paras started college. Whether it was the sight of the first three buttons left unbuttoned on Paras's shirt, or the bike being switched off only after Paras put it on its stand, his father regularly lost his cool.

'But you realize that he loves you, don't you? He's strict only because he thinks you'll become spoilt in bad company at college,' said his mother by way of pacification and explanation. Paras did not find this convincing from either angle.

In his father's opinion, Paras had the unenviable talent of consistently making the wrong choice, despite being provided a life filled with opportunities made possible only through his father's toil and diligence. Granted, said his father, he could not afford to admit Paras to Don Bosco School, where the fees per annum were more than what his entire education had cost. But even Kanhaiya Lal Memorial School *was* a school and Bisalpur Residency College a recognized college affiliated to a big name like Lucknow University. What mattered was how much you studied, how devoted you were to learning and books; it was immaterial how smart or fancy your school uniform was, or how big the college cafeteria.

Paras may have recognized the inherent truth in his father's views, but now that he had a stick to beat his father with, he was not about to let it go. 'The teachers and lecturers there hardly know anything themselves. They passed out from the same school and college and couldn't get jobs anywhere else. What can they teach? What can I learn there? They can't even speak two correct sentences in English. Why, the Political Science lecturer did not know that Holland and The Netherlands were the same country!'

'And you knew?' his father asked, surprised.

'No, but that's not the point. If only you had put me in Don Bosco, how different I would have turned out.'

Here, both father and son were in total agreement. How Paras had turned out was not what either of them had expected, or hoped for. At twenty, he was at that age when each found the other thoroughly irritating and frustrating. Short of being invisible as a ghost, Paras knew there was nothing he could realistically do to avoid censure from his father, and so he no longer made any effort to humour him. He knew that the sight of him in goggles, pushing his long hair off his face with one hand, texting on his mobile with the other, was bound to drive his father mad, but then he might as well stop breathing.

'You don't know how good you have it. Bike, mobile, pocket money. When I was your age....'

'Yes, I know. We've heard it hundreds of times—how you used to walk 14 kilometres every day just to reach your poor thatched school and back.'

'But look where I am today!' his father thundered.

'Where?' asked Paras, in a whisper audible only to his mother who had long ago given up interfering in the father–son quarrels. 'You think earning 30,000 rupees a month at the end of your career is a great achievement?'

His mother frowned at him, while his sister giggled. As Paras got ready to leave, his father yelled, 'What did he say? And why don't you take Priya with you on the bike? Do you think I gave you the bike to show off to other girls but not care about your own sister?'

Paras was already out the door and pretended he hadn't heard his father. He also gunned his bike to make sure he did not hear anything else his father hurled at him. He'd done his best to convince his father not to send Priya to Bisalpur Residency, but in vain. He was certainly not going to lug her to college and back every day on his bike. So what if he did not have a girlfriend—he'd rather go alone than have a family member riding pillion at every turn. Priya could easily take a cycle-rickshaw for five rupees.

The bike itself was another sore point. He'd wanted a Karizma, oozing raw power and style, instead of a boring Splendor. Who bought a bike for just mileage? He'd begged for at least a Yamaha, if his father was that concerned about the price. But of course, as far as his father went, the very fact that the son had been provided a bike was a luxury—a fact that he never tired of reminding Paras about. His father had bought his first vehicle, a Bajaj Chetak scooter, years after his marriage; until then he and his wife had managed their transportation needs quite comfortably using bicycles, cycle-rickshaws and buses.

Once on the road, however, and racing away from home, Paras felt his frustration seeping away. The rhythmic throb of the engine was more soothing than a masseur's touch, allowing him to relax and let his mind wander. Rudy on his Karizma—now that was a cool bike and a cool guy; Paras could not think of another combination as well-paired. Though there were half a dozen contenders still with Rudy on the TV show *The Real Deal*, the world knew that Rudy stood head and shoulders above the rest. A six-foot physique, awe-inspiring biceps and abs to match—a worthy successor to the likes of Hrithik Roshan or John Abraham. You saw that in the shameless way the girls threw themselves at him, or in the fan comments on the show's website. And the palpable envy of the other guys only confirmed the universal opinion that Rudy was the most deserving candidate to win *The Real Deal*, Season Four, by virtue of being the last man standing. Rudy was bound for Bollywood.

As he reached college, Paras spotted Gajanan and his sidekicks at the tea-stall outside the main gate. He couldn't help laughing. That stupid Gajanan imagined he was just as stylish as Rudy, but surely a single glance at the mirror should have told him he was nowhere near the hero of *The Real Deal*. Gajanan's father was one of the richest men in Bisalpur, but no amount of affluence could place Gajanan on par with Rudy. Five-foot-five was short, period. However, a show of deference to such a scion could do no harm.

Paras greeted him, stopping his bike a little distance away. 'So what's happening?'

'Nothing,' Gajanan said. 'Does anything ever happen in Bisalpur? We might as well sit here and check out the girls.'

'What a waste of time,' Paras said.

'As if you spend all the time you save on books. Hell, I get better marks than you!'

Paras wished the others would stop howling with laughter each time Gajanan made a remark, the sycophants. He badly wanted to retort that Gajanan got passing marks because no lecturer wanted to get into his or his father's bad books. But he had to be careful not to rub Gajanan the wrong way, and passed it off as a joke. 'Yes, you get better marks, sometimes without even writing the exam.'

This being taken as a tribute to his power, Gajanan was gratified. A cycle-rickshaw stopped at the entrance, and two girls alighted. One of the sidekicks called out, 'Hey, no books to college?' The remark was ignored and the guy who made the comment was buried in an avalanche of mockery by the others.

'So where should we spend our time? Please enlighten us, Paras Nath.' Gajanan returned to the earlier thread of conversation. Paras hated him for using the abhorred name. Gajanan obviously made it a point, knowing it nettled him. 'We know you don't spend it studying.'

'Cramming textbooks and getting top grades won't make you famous,' retorted Paras, 'unless you are a genius and win a Nobel Prize or something. If you are that good, you wouldn't be studying at Bisalpur Residency for sure. The only things worth one's time are those that can make one famous and one's name known to the world.'

An awkward silence followed for a moment or two, before Gajanan broke it. 'He talks as if he is a great philosopher, but he is actually just a little shit from Bisalpur like all of us.'

Paras accepted the judgement with a grin, parked his bike and joined the group. He didn't have any better alternative to suggest. The euphoria of escaping from home was usually short-lived, lasting while he rode the bike, and ending when confronted by the question of what to do next.

After several excruciatingly dull minutes spent checking out the girls walking into college, not one of whom looked remotely remarkable, Paras was bored. 'No classes today? Are we going to spend the whole day here?'

'No classes. Don't you know there's a strike?'

'Strike? What for?' Paras was mildly surprised, for strikes were a none-too-rare occurrence.

'I called it,' Gajanan explained, 'because I didn't feel like attending classes today.'

Paras could not help but admire such irrefutable logic. Perhaps if his father were that influential, he would have done the same too.

The problem with Bisalpur was that you ran out of options so quickly. When signs of the new economy showed up at the town's doors—a multiplex, a mall, a Coffee Day, a Nokia outlet, a pizza parlour on Mall Road—the entire city was excited. But it soon became clear that the town was getting ahead of itself and had bitten off more than it could chew. The flow of visitors to the mall, the glitzy new shops, and the restaurants on Mall Road quickly reduced to a trickle. What everyone suspected was confirmed, Bisalpur had not changed—it was a pretender. Apart from Mall Road, the major part of the town was like a maze of mirrors in a barber shop—the same streets and colonies and houses reflected and repeated ad nauseum.

'Rudy will win, won't he?' someone in the group asked.

Paras was surprised; he thought he was the only one who followed the show. 'Sure he'll win. He is the best,' he said emphatically. 'He has to win.'

'Rudy who?' asked Gajanan.

'The *Real Deal* guy,' said the sidekick who'd spoken earlier. 'Rudy's the one who thinks he is the stud,' he explained.

'Oh, him,' sneered Gajanan. 'I don't know why you guys even watch that show. It's a different world there.'

'The bikes, the places, the girls...hot stuff!' Paras said.

'That's what I said, a different world, the big-city metro world.'

'Not that far away,' said Paras. 'Delhi is only 350 kilometres from here.'

'Might as well be on the other side of the world. Do you think any of us can even reach the interview stage on that show, forget participating or winning it?'

'Why not? Vikas from Jaunpur made it.'

'What made it? He got booted out in the first vote-out.' Gajanan was in earnest now, but so was Paras. He would normally never drag out an argument with Gajanan for fear of ending up on his wrong side, but Gajanan had brought up the topic of *The Real Deal* and Paras just could not let go. 'He didn't know how to play it, otherwise he would have gone much farther.'

'He just didn't fit in. That was obvious. All the metro guys and girls ganged up against him.'

The bugger followed the show all right, but pretended not to. 'He should have known that,' Paras retorted. 'He didn't play his cards right.'

'Sounds like you know everything about the show. Show us you can get there, then talk. Otherwise you're just full of hot air.' Gajanan was furious now and Paras thought it wiser to back off.

'I'll have to run away from home, because my father would never let me go to such a show even if I qualified.'

A bit mollified, Gajanan said, 'And your great Rudy won't win, I bet.'

'Why not? He is the best.'

'I agree, but others will get jealous, play politics and vote him out. Mark my words.'

Those words had the effect of shutting Paras up as abruptly as a tap turned off. Rudy? Being voted out? He hadn't thought of that possibility. If it happened it would be so unfair, the vilest travesty of justice. Maybe Gajanan was only goading him. Some day, if it ever came about, if he indeed qualified for the show, the look on Gajanan's face would be reward enough. The look on all their faces, in fact—his father, mother, sister (but she would be truly happy for him), his friends. These sycophantic cronies of Gajanan would then flit to him as easily as butterflies from one flower to the next.

He felt his pulse quicken at the thought of straddling a Karizma, with a girl like Komal, in a T-shirt and cut-off jeans, seated behind, her arms around him. And all of it telecast on TV, watched eagerly and enviously by millions while he took off on his bike with as much style and panache as Rudy. He only wished he were a couple of inches taller. And at that he had to laugh; it wasn't as though his height was the only factor that stood between him and his dreams.

'Hey, who's that?'

Paras looked up and saw a girl riding a red bike, the indicator signalling that she intended turning into their college. The sight was so incongruous that it spontaneously evoked a chorus of whistles, some soft, some full-throated, from their group. Girls riding Kinetics and scooties, though earlier a rarity in Bisalpur, had ceased having shock value over the last couple of years. But a girl riding a bike like a Yamaha SZ 150cc belonged to the rarest-of-the-rare category. To add to it, the girl was dressed in a T-shirt and jeans. Girls on scooties in a modest salwar-kameez with a dupatta wrapped around their faces to ward off the dust and prying eyes—that was as far as Bisalpur was prepared to accept the emancipation of women.

Sitting behind her, riding pillion, was another girl in more conventional attire—salwar-kameez complete with wrapped-around dupatta.

Embarrassed by the fact that his bike was truly mediocre compared to hers, Paras tried to hide the Splendor behind him as she approached the college gates. It became clear then that the girl was not used to riding the bike. It wobbled, almost stalled, recovered, then bucked and dipped like a horse, before finally recovering again amid the screams and laughter of the two girls. At that moment, the dupatta slid off the face of the girl sitting behind and with a shock Paras recognized his sister. Only when the duo had turned out of sight behind the administration building, did the speechless boys find their tongues.

'Wow! Who was that?' said Gajanan.

'Sulochana Gupta,' another sidekick furnished helpfully, 'second year, Political Science.'

'She isn't new, you mean?' Paras asked. 'How come I never noticed her before?'

'It's the first time she has come in a bike, perhaps that's why.' The sidekick was reputed to have information on almost all the girls in college and his knowledge was never doubted.

'The girl behind was not too bad either,' someone else spoke up.

'Bastard, that's my sister,' Paras said. 'Bite your tongue.'

'Oops! Sorry.'

Gajanan roared with laughter. 'That Sulochana might be someone's sister too. That didn't stop you from leching at her. Anyway, she's your sister's friend. I would use that trump card if I were you.'

Paras did not need Gajanan to tell him that. He would collar his sister at home later and extract all the information he needed. To Gajanan, he said, 'Not interested. Not my type, really. I don't care.'

The excitement of the incident ebbed over the following hour as the sun grew hotter. Empty teacups were set aside and cigarette butts ground into the dust. The news of the strike also seemed to have got around as hardly anyone turned up thereafter. Now everybody fidgeted, waiting for Gajanan to give the word. Eventually, he stirred and said, 'Okay, it's getting boring now. Let's go.'

'Go where?' Paras asked. Not deigning to reply, Gajanan jumped on to his Karizma and gunned it. Though Paras was saddled with a Splendor possibly for life, Gajanan changed bikes like he would a pair of shoes. When he joined college he rode a CBZ, replacing that with a Karizma, and now he was wondering aloud and often whether to get a Hunk or a Yamaha FZ, perhaps oblivious of how deprived it made the others feel.

The gang was expected to follow, wherever he went. When Gajanan roared off with his entourage, Paras cursed and tailed them, unable to think of anything better to do. He went at his own pace, knowing there was no chance his Splendor could catch up with Gajanan's Karizma.

They screamed and hollered as they drove down Mall Road to attract attention. But by now they were all too familiar a sight to succeed. People simply went about their own business, or acknowledged them with a shake of their heads and a scowl. Paras, at the tail-end of the group, felt silly and soon gave up such forced attempts at showing off his machismo.

At the end of Mall Road, they came across two cops laughing over a relaxed cup of tea, amicably extorted from a roadside vendor. Their big Enfield stood nearby, probably the only bike owned by the Bisalpur police force. For reasons best known to him, Gajanan veered close, paused for a moment, shot his leg out and toppled the bike before vrooming away. What was fun for Gajanan was usually a risky affair for the rest.

The policemen swore and righted the bike and set off in pursuit. But Gajanan had too much of a start. The cops, realizing they could not catch the actual culprit, nabbed the straggler in the gang—Paras. As soon as he pulled over, one of them cuffed him in the face.

'What did I do?' said Paras, stung.

'Who kicked the bike down, motherfucker?'

'You know it was not me.'

'Who was it then? Tell us the name.'

'Gajanan Choradiya.' Paras did not have any qualms about revealing the name. Gajanan would be able to take care of himself, and why should he suffer for no fault of his?

'Choradiya? Kamala Lal Choradiya's son?'

Paras nodded. The cops looked at each other.

'You come with us to the station.'

'What for? I didn't do anything!'

One of them swiftly removed the key from Paras's bike, 'Pull the bike along and come to the station. We have to recover the damage to our bike. It's government property. We are registering a case.'

'So file it against Gajanan. What did I do?'

For that, Paras received another sound cuff on his head.

'If you have any sense, you'll know how to get your bike back and not ask stupid questions. We know your bike's number, so don't try anything smart.' And jingling the keys to Paras's bike, the cops drove away.

CHAPTER 2

Their stunned disbelief had been worth stealing out of the house and risking her mother's ire, decided Sulochana. They hung idly about the tea-stall every morning, smoking (since there was a No Smoking rule inside campus), and had been unable to conceal their astonishment today. They might try to put on sophisticated airs, but the college guys were all Bisalpuri at heart, unable to reconcile to the sight of a girl in jeans and a T-shirt riding a big bike.

Since she'd wanted to shock the whole college, she'd felt a bit flat when she found out about the flash strike. All that effort to get away from home on the bike, in jeans, in vain. But then, she would have missed the look on the guys' faces if she hadn't done it.

Priya had stayed back in case some dedicated lecturer, undeterred by the strike, decided to take classes. She said she'd go home in a rickshaw, and Sulochana was fine with that because she didn't want to stay back in college for nothing. She would zip around the town instead. She needed the practice. While starting the bike and slowing down, she had to be careful not to let the bike lean too much one way or the other, and overwhelm her with its weight. She also had to get used to shifting the gears smoothly, otherwise the boys would think she didn't know how to drive. Once the bike started, she didn't have to worry about the balance; she was comfortable.

The most difficult part was kickstarting it.

The electronic start-up didn't work, and her father had probably never bothered to get it repaired, considering it too girly a feature to use. He had taught her how to use her body weight to jump on the starter pedal, while taking care not to slip and hurt herself. She had been so angry with her mother in the morning because she had had to tiptoe out of the house with the bike. Now her anger abated. If it was so hard for her to come to terms with her father's death, how much harder must it be for her mother to accept it?

Her mood darkened as it always did at the thought of her father. And he always came to mind whenever she kickstarted the bike. She ought to be able to remember him now without a lump in the throat. Bad things happened to good people. So for no fault of his, her father had died in an accident caused by a reckless car driver.

What was the point in continuing to mourn three years on? Three years ought to be long enough to recover from tragedy. She ought to be rational about the whole matter, as though it were something she'd read in the newspaper, something that had happened to someone unknown. Hundreds died every day—disasters, accidents, disease, bullets, bombs, even hunger and thirst. What was the point of asking again and again, 'Why him?' or 'Why me?' when so many others had the right to the same question?

She drove out of the exit gate, the guys at the entrance following her with their eyes. She knew heads would turn and gape wherever she went. But the comforting hum of the powerful engine gave her strength to drive on.

Sulochana dismissed the thought of returning home—the day had barely begun, and she was starting to get the hang of the bike. Besides, there would be an inevitable scene at home. Her mother would have noticed her absence and the bike's as well—the accursed bike that had killed her husband and miraculously escaped unscathed but for a few scratches, its red body blending with the spattered blood of its owner. Even the rearview mirrors were intact. If her mother had had her way, she would have sold the bike off as scrap the day after the funeral. To Sulochana, the bike was a bittersweet memento of her father.

As she drove, she felt the protective strength of her father's arms enveloping her own across the handlebars. When he'd sat behind her and let her take control of the handles, she'd never feared falling. Her father would never let anything bad happen to her. How easily he'd laughed her mother's worries off, without ever getting angry.

'Careful! She'll get hurt, she's a girl. What's she going to do by learning to ride a motorcycle? What are people going to say? You wanted a boy, didn't you?'

'I am here, how can she get hurt? The world has other things to do besides worrying about me teaching my daughter to ride a bike. And, mark my word, she will ride a bike better than any boy. She's better than any boy I could have ever wanted.'

Even as they laughed at her together, Sulochana knew her mother was not really angry or worried. Those conversations between her parents, arising from and reinforced over the bike lessons, were like a secret between them.

So after her father's death, Sulochana had put her foot down and wailed that it would be the end of her if the bike was sold. Already distraught, her mother was not in the frame of mind to oppose her and had let her have her way. Like its owner, the bike had lain as good as dead, because there was no one to ride it. Sulochana had wanted to, but now it was her mother's turn to put her foot down. 'You didn't let me sell it. But no one in this house is ever going to ride that cursed bike again.' So it stood idle, gathering dust and cobwebs for months. If the clothesline outside was full, or if it was raining, it served as a clothes-stand as well. It became an anonymous, stationary piece of furniture.

On the day before Diwali the following year, her mother, on her brother's (Sulochana's Mamaji) advice, decided to observe the festival in a low-key way and the whole house was scrubbed and cleaned. She had skipped Diwali the previous year in the wake of her husband's death, but skipping festivals forever would cast a pall on the children—so went her brother's advice, encouraging her to try to return the family to normality.

With the whole house sparkling clean, Sulochana felt bad the bike had been left untouched. It stuck out like a sore thumb so she washed and polished it until it gleamed. Her mother pretended not to notice. Thereafter, Sulochana gained ground inch by inch. The bike was washed monthly and then weekly. Soon she was taking the bike off its stand and sitting on it, her fingers gripping the handlebars. She could almost feel her father sitting behind her, teaching her how to maintain balance, change the gears smoothly while releasing the clutch...

Then one day, when her mother was out for a few hours at a bhajan prayer programme in the neighbourhood, she dragged the bike out of the house and tried to start it. Her kid sister Sulakshana protested, but in vain. Sulochana didn't have to listen to her, so she didn't. She tried her best to recall her father's lessons, jumping up and down on the starter pedal, but the bike had lain dormant for too long and remained unyielding despite persistent efforts. Sweat streamed down her face. Sulakshana stood in the doorway and watched. Sulochana stepped on the pedal and her foot slipped; the pedal sprung back and hit her shin. She cried out in pain, clutching her leg.

'Let it be, Didi,' Sulakshana said. 'Maybe we are not meant to start it.' Sulochana refused to buy that and resumed stomping on the pedal, to no avail. Pausing to recover her strength between kicks, she vaguely recalled her father's tip to turn the choke knob the other way if the bike refused to start. But the engine remained as lifeless as ever.

There was still a little petrol left; she had heard it splash around in the tank when she moved the bike, so fuel was not the problem. The battery must be dead, since the bike had been unused for over a year. There had to be some other way. She suddenly remembered how her father had once started the bike without using either the electric start or by kick-starting.

She almost believed he could work magic on the bike until, laughing at her awestruck face, he had let her on to the push-start method.

'Sulakshna, come,' Sulochana said. She took the bike off its stand and straddled it, shifting to the second gear. 'Now push the bike as hard as you can,' she said, holding the clutch in. Sulakshana complied reluctantly, struggling to throw her small weight behind the bulky bike, while Sulochana tried to assist her by using her feet to propel the bike forward. The gentle slope of the road helped her gather a little momentum. But it was only on her third attempt at releasing and engaging the clutch while increasing the throttle that the engine finally sputtered to life.

Sulochana looked back triumphantly at her sister, who stood panting and mopping her forehead, sharing her joy with a smile. She let the engine run for a few minutes, then turned around slowly and put it back in its place in the veranda of her house.

Once she had been able to resurrect the bike, it was simply a matter of time and opportunity (provided by her mother's infrequent absences). Sulochana began to make swift progress. She realized early on that her salwar suit was not conducive to motorbike riding. That meant her only pair of jeans—intended to be worn only if and when she ever was in Delhi—had to come out of the closet. The first time she actually rode the bike, she had to take it to one of the only two petrol pumps in town. There she had been embarrassed to find that she did not know where the petrol tank was, until the attendant pointed it out and opened the tank lid for her.

Smiling at these memories and zooming down towards Mall Road, Sulochana reflected that the one good thing about a place like Bisalpur was that the roads were not choked with traffic, the way they were in Delhi and other big cities. Riding was a breeze, as long as you alerted others by honking like mad. Only one road in town, the Mall Road, was wide enough to require a divider separating opposing streams of traffic.

She turned into Mall Road and her heart leaped into her mouth as she drove past a traffic cop. She did not have a driving licence. Perhaps her air of confidence had deterred the cop from halting her and checking her papers. Exhilarated, Sulochana spurred the bike on, revving up the accelerator.

She would need to get a driving licence, now that she was going to use the bike regularly. There were enough agents to get that done for a fee, without her even having to visit the RTO. And a pair of goggles to prevent the sand from blowing into her eyes. A helmet would crush her hair, but a scarf was a must unless she wanted her hair to end up looking as matted and dirty as a Naga Sadhu's. What good would it be to hide behind the mask of a helmet anyway?

Sulochana was forced to halt at the only traffic signal in town, which had been put up more out of form than necessity. The instant it turned green the car driver behind her honked, as though waiting a millisecond more was a crime. She tried to switch gears too quickly and the bike jumped and jerked to a stop. The driver honked impatiently, finding his path obstructed. Cursing, Sulochana got off and dragged the bike to the side with difficulty.

'Why ride such a big bike when you can't handle it?' came the parting shot from the window of the departing car.

'Need any help?' Three guys on the sidewalk had stopped, obviously attracted by the novel sight that Sulochana provided. Sulochana kept quiet, knowing their altruistic offer was not to be taken at face value. Bisalpur was full of such unemployed young men who had too much time to kill, and nothing worthwhile to do. They sniggered as she jumped up and down on the starter.

'That's a new way to start the bike.'

'Careful! If the bike falls over, we won't be able to find you under it.'

As she continued ignoring them, their comments grew more suggestive and innuendo-laden.

'Meet Rampur ki Sita. Or rather, Bisalpur ki Sita.'

'Which era are you living in, man? This is Bisalpur ki Mallika Sherawat.'

A dozen retorts came readily to her tongue but Sulochana managed to hold her peace. Just let the damn bike start, and she would show these lowlifes their place. Her prayers were answered. The engine spluttered, and came to life after two more kicks.

She sat firmly on the saddle and checked that the engine ran with a reassuring steadiness. Just before setting off, she turned back at the guys and yelled, 'Go to hell, sisterfuckers!'

'If I had a sister like you, then...' but by the time the stunned guys had come up with a retort, she was far away, the faint residue of their imprecations drowned out by the bike. Her anger soon gave way to exultation. It was beautiful, this heady sensation of liberation and power the bike gave her. She should have tried it long ago. If her mother thought she could snatch the bike away from her, she was badly mistaken.

A group of bikers was heading towards her from the opposite direction. They looked like her college mates who had witnessed her entry at the college gates earlier. Yes, that was Gajanan at their head, she recognized, as they roared past, every single guy turning around to look at her, as though saluting a dignitary at a parade.

She envied the guys their freedom. They did not have to worry what their parents would say, and here she was feeling indignant and guilty about indulging in a simple pleasure that harmed no one.

Ten minutes later, Sulochana discovered she had completed a full circuit of the town. All of it. Now, either she began another round, or drove out of Bisalpur altogether, and on to the highway. Both options were unappealing; she chose to return home instead and plan her next escapade at leisure.

A deathly quiet hung in the air as she wheeled in the bike through the gate and put it on its main stand with some difficulty. For a moment, Sulochana thought her mother had not returned from her bhajan programme and the house was empty, but then the door would have been locked. Though Sulakshana had gone to school, her mother was very much in.

'What do you think you are doing?' her mother asked, looking her up and down.

There was nothing to say.

'You went out on the bike, didn't you?'

Again, the question did not merit a reply, apart from a brief nod, given that she had just dragged in the bike.

'And what are you wearing? Have you no shame?'

Finally something to respond to. 'What's wrong with my clothes?'

'What's wrong?' her mother echoed, incredulous. 'Since when have you begun wearing jeans and T-shirts, like a boy? Are we in Delhi or what?'

'I don't care.'

'I do.' Then, in a quieter and injured tone, 'I know you are doing it because your father isn't here. Otherwise you would not have dared.'

'Don't bring Papa into this. If he were here...' Sulochana found her voice quavering. 'If he were here, he would encourage me. He was the one who taught me how to ride the bike.'

'It was okay when he was there; no one could say anything. Not now, when there is no man in the house. We have to be careful. You are old enough to understand that, Sulo.'

'Well then, someone has to be the man of the house. We cannot hide inside the house all the time.'

Her mother was taken aback by her belligerence and fell silent. Then she said in more conciliatory tones, 'You can be the man of the house without having to wear a man's clothes. Do what you want quietly, without attracting attention.'

'It's not my fault if others notice.'

'What kind of an example are you setting your younger sister? She is still in school. She looks up to you for everything.'

'Look, Mamma, nothing has happened. I just went out on the bike to college and came back. There is no need to make such a big deal out of it,' said Sulochana, walking away to her room to mark the end of the conversation from her side.

If she stuck to her stand, her mother would have no option but to fall in, or she would never be able to have her way. Sulochana surveyed herself in the long mirror affixed to the door of the wardrobe. Compared to the girls on *The Real Deal*, she was so modestly dressed; in Delhi, no one would even give her a second glance. Didn't her mother ever notice what the girls wore on TV, such short skirts that when they sat on a couch, they had to hold a cushion over their legs to project a semblance of propriety? Tank tops and low-waist jeans that left exposed navels equidistant from both? Pierced bellybuttons; tattooed backs. And look at her! Even in the jeans and T-shirt that had so shocked her mother and all the guys in Bisalpur, she was just a poor country cousin in front of girls on the show, like Komal.

Sulochana made sure that the door was bolted before she opened the wardrobe. From an inner recess—the existence of which she had guarded for so long that her mother had forgotten about it—from under a stack of respectable salwar suits, she picked out a midriff-baring scarlet top and torn-off denim shorts. She had bought them in Delhi when she had gone with her uncle to file a college application last year. She had found an opportunity to slip out to a mall near the hotel and bought them with the money her mother had given her for exigencies. That college admission had never materialized.

Now, in her room, she put them on and subjected herself anew to another critical assessment in the mirror. This time, she could pass muster as one of the hep girls on *The Real Deal*. Her tummy was flat enough but her hairstyle, rather the lack of it, was glaringly obvious. Long and straight and...nothing else. She ought to get it cut, perhaps make it a bit wavy, add some lustre and bounce, and give it some personality.

She struck a pose, one elbow on her hip. 'Fuck,' she said carefully, then whispered 'shit' and giggled. That girl Komal was unbelievable—such a pretty, delicate face, but the way she cursed caught everyone by surprise.

The curtains on the window fluttered and Sulochana thought she saw someone outside. She crept quietly to the window and peeped. A young man, vaguely familiar, stood on the street in front of her house. He looked puzzled, taking a few hesitant steps this way and that, as though searching for something or someone. His long hair kept falling over his eyes and he kept brushing it back. Was he one of the guys who had been teasing her and whom she had roundly abused before fleeing on the bike? Had he somehow tracked her down? The bike, standing parked before him in plain sight, was a giveaway.

Then, abruptly decisive, he walked away with quick steps up the street. Sulochana relaxed and then it came to her—she knew who he was! She had seen him in the morning at the college gates in Gajanan's group, and probably on other occasions too. He was Priya's brother.

CHAPTER 3

Paras was distraught now that his bike had been confiscated by the cops. It was not so much that he had to tell his father about it, but being deprived of the bike felt like an amputation. How had he survived without it earlier? Even if his mother wanted a box of matches from the corner store he would reach for his bike, much to everyone's exasperation. If there was one act of his father's that he was silently grateful for, that was getting him the Splendor, even if it was a make that every second person in the country had.

Telling his father was unavoidable; he could not simply shrug away the loss of the bike. But his father would never accept that it was all his fault. Had he been less stingy with pocket money, Paras could have found a 100-rupee note in his pocket to appease the policemen with. That was all it would have taken, one note, to end the matter there and then to everybody's satisfaction. The cops would have felt somewhat compensated for their bike being kicked down in public, and Paras would not have had his bike taken from him. But all he'd had were two five-rupee coins. He knew better than to offer that to the cops. Maybe the cops would be more amenable to dealing with an adult than a rebellious college kid. So, while trudging home on foot, he tried to come up with ways to persuade his father to go to the police station to reclaim the bike.

'Bhaiya! Paras!'

Startled out of his reverie by his sister's voice, Paras looked up and found her beckoning him from a rickshaw. She was on her way home from college after reluctantly accepting the fact that there would be no classes that day. Paras hopped in beside her, evoking a spontaneous objection from the rickshaw-wala, 'Do sawari. Ten rupees!'

'Think big, beyond money. Always haggling about five and ten rupees.'

'For us, Bhaiya,' retorted the rickshaw-wala, 'these are big amounts.'

'All right, all right.' Paras dismissed him. Meeting his sister had reminded him of the other incident of the morning, which the brush with the cops had temporarily erased from his mind.

'Where's your cycle?' he asked.

'And where's your bike?' came the sisterly reply.

'Forget mine,' said Paras. 'Long story, but it is with the police now.'

'Police?' Priya was aghast. 'What did you do?'

'Nothing. Forget it. Nothing serious, anyway. Papa will be mad for two days, that's all.'

'But—'

'Who were you with on the bike in the morning?'

'Oh, you saw.' Priya smiled happily.

Paras felt his heart flood with affection for his kid sister. Sometimes he raged at himself for not being able to do more for her, for not being a better role model as an elder brother ought to be, and at other times, he simply forgot all about her. He knew she always defended him in front of their parents, no matter what he did—failing exams, or insisting on his dire need for a good-quality willow cricket bat, even if it was prohibitively expensive. If any guy even tried to look at her the wrong way, he would gouge out the bastard's eyes.

'I know everything,' he said. 'Who was she?'

'Who, Sulochana?'

'Yes, Sulochana. So you know her well?'

'Not that well. Same year, but not in the same class. Why?'

'Nothing. Does she always ride a bike and dress that way?'

'That's the first time I saw her like that.' Priya looked at him, eyes narrowed. 'Why so much interest in her, Bhaiya?'

'You don't see girls like that in Bisalpur every day.'

'Hmm.' Priya was silent for a minute. Paras knew she was dying to ask about his interest in Sulochana, but that was something even he was not clear about. The street was strangely silent, apart from the creaking of the rickshaw wheels, and the panting of the rickshaw-wala as he toiled up a gentle incline. Priya was free to think what she liked.

'Her house is in that colony.'

Paras looked towards where she was pointing. 'There?'

'The house with the blue gate, I think.'

'Stop.' Paras told the rickshaw-wala. 'I'll get down here.'

'What are you going to do?'

'But we agreed on ten rupees,' said the rickshaw-wala.

'Yes baba!' said Paras in exasperation. 'Think big, remember? Priya, give him ten rupees. And you go home. I'll come soon.'

'Should I wait?'

'Waiting charges are extra,' said the rickshaw-wala.

'No! Just go home.'

The moment Priya had pointed out Sulochana's house, Paras felt bound to complete the picture for himself—not just establish where she lived, but to also find out who she lived with, who her neighbours were, what kind of a locality it was. Priya, thankfully, was not a snitch and could be counted upon to keep her curiosity and observations to herself.

The vision of Sulochana driving up to college that morning played in an endless loop in his mind, like some breaking news clip on a sensational news channel. She had only provided momentary shock value for Gajanan and his gang. She would not linger in their minds as she did in his. Watching girls in jeans and T-shirts, maybe even riding a bike, as in *The Real Deal*, was normal, even expected, on TV. You didn't think they were real, or if they were, they existed in a parallel world you would never be a part of. But when you saw it in the same commonplace world that you lived in, it was all too real, all too close and you could not get rid of it.

Where was the blue gate now? He saw one, but almost immediately another one opposite, and yet another, two houses removed. The first had a nameplate of Varma, the other of Tripathi, and the third did not have any, which therefore could belong to the Guptas. His heart skipped a beat as he recognized the red Yamaha SZ parked beside the wall. It took guts and courage for a girl to do what she had in Bisalpur. Perhaps the town did need a shaking up, or it would never catch up.

Paras sensed a shadow move across a window in the Gupta house. He felt he was being observed and was prepared to swear it was Sulochana spying on him. As suddenly as he had made up his mind to seek out her house, his enthusiasm deserted him. What if she came out and confronted him? What excuse did he have to be there? What exactly did he plan to accomplish through this visit?

Talking about girls was different from talking to them. Paras's interaction with the opposite sex was limited to a question or two about their classes or exams. But he could not knock on her door and start talking about lecturers and notes. This was new ground for him and he needed to be better prepared.

The depressing matter of the loss of his bike returned to haunt him. He had to get that sorted out, or he would be making trips to Sulochana's house on foot like a true pilgrim.

'Isn't Paras home yet?' Paras heard his father ask his mother. More than an hour had passed since his father returned from office. But it was an hour that he had made clear long ago was sacrosanct. He needed this hour, he said, to transition from the stress of office to the peace at home. He was to be left strictly alone with his cup of tea, two Marie biscuits and the newspaper. He would not brook any disturbance, queries from his wife regarding the household, or from his children regarding college or any other sundry concerns they might have.

During his childhood, Paras had observed these dictums with unquestioning solemnity. Later, of course, he mocked this 'daily drama'—though only to his mother or sister. 'Oh, come on, he works in the Public Irrigation Department. What kind of stress could he have there? I can't imagine a more relaxing place than that.' But he saw the wisdom in his mother's patient response, 'How does it matter? Just humour him and leave him alone for an hour.'

But now that he had himself asked about his son, Paras decided to emerge from his room and sit on the couch in the drawing room.

His father frowned. 'Where's the bike, if you are here? I told you not to lend it to your friends. No one cares about someone else's property. And you can't go claiming damages from your friends. Just make some excuse. At least, I hope they will fill petrol in it.'

Paras desisted from interrupting him. He wished he could forget all about it, wake up the next morning and find that the bike was back in its usual place in the veranda. 'Actually, Papa, the bike is not with any friend. It's with the police.'

The inevitability of what followed did not make it any the less worse for him. Indeed, he was surprised at the extent to which his predictions tallied with what actually transpired. Father transitioning from shock, to anger, to wrath. Check. Father recounting, one after another, his various misdemeanours and his misfortune in having to rear a son like him. Check. Father threatening him with dire consequences if only to make him realize and appreciate how much he had been spoiled in life. Check.

The best way to weather the storm was to hear him out with a half-bowed head and a contrite word or two in response. But when his father's tirade did not show any sign of abating, Paras had to interrupt him. 'Don't you think we should go to the police station to get the bike back?'

Halted mid-speech, his father looked at him murderously before yelling at his wife to take his work clothes out again. 'Get ready,' he told Paras brusquely.

'Me? They will return the bike to you more easily.'

'Idiot!' his father exploded. 'Can I ride both scooter and motorcycle together? How will I come back with both? Or do you want me to walk to the police station?'

Half an hour later, they reached the police station, and after a further ten minutes inside it, his father emerged wearing a harried look. He tossed the bike keys at Paras. 'Get the bike. We will talk at home.'

After his father had stormed off in a roar and in a cloud of white smoke from his Bajaj Chetak, Paras located his bike parked along with a cluster of other impounded bikes and scooters. The reassuring feel of the handlebars and the seat comforted him. But the bike would not start. How could the fuel gauge needle go that far below zero? He cursed and a constable laughed. The nearest petrol pump was almost a mile away, and he had the same two five-rupee notes in his pocket that he had had in the morning.

When he reached home forty minutes later, after pleading with the petrol pump attendant to fill ten rupees' worth of fuel, his father was pacing up and down outside the house, looking as dark as an oil-sooted mechanic. 'Now what? Why couldn't you come home straight?'

'The cops had drained the petrol. I had to push it to the pump.'

'Why would they do that?'

'How would I know? Do you think I'm telling a lie?'

'Let him rest,' said his mother. 'Look at him, so tired and sweaty.'

'Wonderful!' snorted his father. 'Sympathy for him and nothing for me for pleading with those corrupt people; for having to shell out 300 rupees of my hard-earned money because this good-for-nothing finds it fun to kick police bikes down.'

'I did not. Gajanan did it.'

'Why keep company with such people then? Concentrate on your studies; how many times have I told you?'

Priya made a face at him behind her father's back. When his father caught him making a face back, he was infuriated. 'Is this a joke? When will you learn to handle your responsibilities?'

'What responsibility? Don't burden me with responsibilities at this age. I have my whole life to carry them out.'

'See how he talks! At your age, I—'

But Paras had had enough. Though both his mother and his inner voice were telling him to exercise restraint, he ignored them. 'Well, I am your responsibility because I am your son.'

'Yes, but not throughout my life,' his father countered without a second's hesitation. 'Only until you turned eighteen; you should have been on your own after that. It's only in India that we pamper and spoil our children even when they have children of their own. You are twenty.'

'Fine! I'll take care of myself.' He turned and stormed to his room as a taunting 'Take care? How?' reached his ears.

In his room, Paras fumed. He yanked out a few shirts and trousers and threw them on the bed. What else would he need? Toothbrush, some underwear, what else? After all, he had not expected his father to take this line of argument.

Priya came into the room. 'What are you doing?'

Paras did not deign to reply.

'Where will you go? Stay? Do you have money? What will you do?'

The momentum of his anger had carried him as far as dumping his clothes on the bed, but no further.

'So what should I do? Listen to every insult he throws at me?' he asked.

'Just calm down. Do nothing. Everything will be okay tomorrow.'

'But—'

'He's just angry at having to shell out 300 rupees without warning. Tomorrow morning say sorry to him and he'll forget everything.'

'*I* should say sorry?'

'Do you want the bike back or not?'

Paras had to smile. 'Since when did you become so clever, little girl?'

Paras went according to plan and avoided his father for the rest of the evening and also the next morning until he was about to leave for work. Then, seizing his moment, he went up to him and quietly apologized for the previous day's events. Surprised, his father nodded but did not say anything.

As soon as his father left, Paras did a celebratory jig before getting ready for college.

'Where are the keys?' he asked his mother, not finding them at their usual place on the wall. A thorough but futile search ensued, leading to the inescapable conclusion that his father had taken the keys with him. Paras felt gutted, cheated.

'Say sorry and everything will be okay!' He threw Priya a scornful look.

'Maybe he took the keys by mistake,' she said.

'Hah!'

Nevertheless, Paras decided to give his father the benefit of doubt but when the keys failed to return to their place the next morning, he understood it was no oversight but punishment being meted out to him. He resolved not to give his father the satisfaction of knowing he was suffering—his father had chosen to hit him where it hurt but he was not going to show the pain.

The next day, he accompanied Priya to college on a rickshaw as though he did it every day. His only response when Priya or members of Gajanan's gang mentioned the bike was a shrug. This stoic approach was not put on. The bike and the keys simply didn't matter; they'd been overshadowed by Sulochana.

Sulochana was not like the other girls in college, who believed in not standing out and made efforts to blend into the background. Nothing the guys did or said provoked them from their statue-like passivity, for fear of being deemed of questionable character. But not Sulochana. And it was this fire in her that had him hooked.

Desperate to catch a glimpse of her in college, but failing to find her, Paras knew he had to revisit the street Sulochana lived in. Again, as on the previous day, he found the Yamaha parked just outside the door with no one around. He was again at a loss as to what to do next. He was still looking stupidly at the bike when the door opened and out came Sulochana, dressed in a modest salwar suit with a red dupatta.

'Were you looking for someone?' she asked.

Though petrified for a moment, he realized this was his chance. 'This is the Avasthi house, right?' He had planned the excuse overnight.

'Avasthi? No, I don't think there is any Avasthi in this row at least.'

'Oh, okay. Maybe I should look in the next street then.'

'Maybe.'

But neither did Paras make any move to withdraw, nor did Sulochana. It was the first time he was seeing her up-close. Barring a tiny scar on her forehead, her face was flawless, the complexion a shade fairer than what would be described as 'wheatish' in a matrimonial advertisement.

'You are Priya's brother, aren't you?'

Paras flashed a big smile, mostly of relief. 'You know her?'

'Sure, same year. So you must be our senior then.'

'I suppose so.'

'Just yesterday,' she said, her excitement making her flush, 'I gave Priya a lift.'

'Aah. So you were the girl on the bike yesterday?'

Sulochana giggled. 'So you saw us?'

'Of course. You think a girl in jeans riding a big bike will go unnoticed in Bisalpur?' Paras moved a step closer, so that the blue gate stood as the sole barrier between them. 'That was brave of you, you know.'

'Really, you think so? Everyone looks at you so strangely merely for riding a bike, just because you are a girl, as if you have done something shameful.'

'Most people in Bisalpur are assholes.' Paras was spontaneous in his reassurance, and then mortified because he'd used a profanity.

Her eyes met his. 'So you know what Bisalpur is like?'

Paras nodded, not trusting himself to speak, his heart bubbling over with dread and excitement. He realized he was looking into the eyes of a soulmate. Barely a minute of talking had been enough to establish an understanding between them; his growing-up years at home had only convinced him that he lived on a planet different from the one his parents inhabited.

Nothing in his experience had taught him to speak to a girl like that, but somehow, instinctively, he was confident that no matter what, she would understand.

'Wish I had a bike like that,' Paras said, renewing the conversation that had suddenly ceased.

'Don't you have a bike?'

'I have, but my father has taken it away from me as a punishment.' There was no need to lie to her.

'Punishment?' she laughed. 'Why? What did you do?'

'Nothing. You know how fathers are. They just like to torment their children for no reason except to show who's in charge.'

'Don't say that!' The edge in her voice took him by surprise. 'Not all fathers are like that.'

'Well, not all I guess. Your father must be a good man.'

'He was. He was the one who taught me how to ride the bike.'

'Was—?' Paras searched her face. She nodded, her cheeks a bit puffed as though she was holding herself from bursting into tears. 'I am sorry.' How was he to know?

'Sulochana!' A woman's sharp voice rang out from inside the house. 'Where are you?'

Sulochana came to, with a start. 'I must go,' she said softly. Paras felt delighted at the conspiratorial whispering.

'You will come to college on your bike, then?' he asked, unwilling to let her go.

'Yes, but I can't give you a lift, only your sister,' she said, giggling.

Paras felt his throat go dry. 'Can I tell you one thing? You looked good on the bike. There's a reality show on YTV, *The Real Deal*, don't know if you watch it. There—'

'My favourite show, never miss an episode.'

What more proof did he need that she was his soulmate? 'Then you must know Komal. You remind me of her.'

'Komal! But she's so classy. You mean I—'

'Sulochana!' The tone was much sharper this time. Sulochana rushed in, waving a hasty goodbye in his direction before shutting the door.

Paras left in a daze. Just a few minutes ago he could count on the fingers of one hand the total number of words he had spoken to any girl at college. And now he had established a connection with the most spirited and beautiful girl in college, during his first conversation with her, and this could only be the harbinger of something even better...what, he dared not imagine.

It was this all-enveloping daze that rendered him immune to the loss of his bike, or to the occasional joke cracked by Gajanan and company at his expense.

But even the loss of his bike proved temporary. Apparently, Priya had advocated his cause, finding their father in an approachable mood. His father allowed himself to be convinced, worried perhaps by Paras's new attitude of silent acceptance. So after three days of going around by foot and rickshaw, Paras found the bike keys back in place. He did not need a second invitation to pocket them.

CHAPTER 4

The first day Sulochana had spotted Priya's brother hanging outside her house, she had been bemused by the coincidence. She had given Priya a ride to the college just that morning. But when she saw him outside her gate the second day in succession, she realized it was no coincidence. He'd looked as confused as on the previous day and seeing her mother busy in the kitchen, Sulochana had stepped out to confront him.

The ensuing conversation had left her amused. His quest for the fictitious Avasthi house was a blatant lie, of course, but she was also moved because of his reaction to the mention of her father. Priya's brother—and she realized then that she did not know his name—was different, even if he had the same outdated, stupid puffed-up, brushed-back hairdo as all the other guys in college. None of them was worth talking to, but she was sure most of them did not hold the opinion that Bisalpur was provincial. His comparison of her with Komal of *The Real Deal* was flattering and carried a ring of truth, which would not have been the case had he attempted an outrageous comparison with some Bollywood starlet.

The next day she saw him hanging out with the bunch of guys who stationed themselves on their bikes just outside the college gates every morning. Perhaps he had always been a part of that idle group but she had never noticed him before. But this time their eyes met, and she granted him a quick smile of recognition, which she was tickled to find reduced him to a blush. Her smile and his reaction did not go unobserved by the other guys, who immediately began nudging, winking and hooting. Sulochana was not surprised—you could not smile at a guy in Bisalpur without it becoming breaking news.

Though more subdued in her reaction, Priya was no less astonished than those guys when Sulochana tried to find out more about her brother.

'Paras Nath,' she said, 'but why?'

'Nothing, just like that,' replied Sulochana and saw that Priya looked unconvinced. She quickly said, 'Hey, I could pick you up on the days I get my bike to college. How about that?'

'That'd be fun,' said Priya, keeping her curiosity to herself.

Paras Nath. No wonder he wasn't keen on telling her his name, Sulochana thought. Anyway, now it was up to him, depending on what, or on how badly, he wanted to talk to her. If he thought she was going to seek him out, he was mistaken.

But as it turned out she did not have to wait long. Paras sought her out in college the next day, trying to be as unobtrusive about it as possible.

'So, didn't get your bike today?' he asked.

'You think I can ride in this?' she asked in turn, indicating her salwar.

'That's why I asked. But why not? You said you'd come on the bike to college every day.'

'Did I? My mother doesn't like my riding the bike or wearing T-shirts.'

'If you keep listening to everyone in Bisalpur, you'll never do anything you like.'

'My mother is not everyone! And how do you know what I like? Why are you so keen I ride my bike?' she asked sharply, relishing his discomfort. 'Maybe I don't like it, maybe I just tried it once to see what was the big deal.'

'You don't fool me. I know you like it.'

'You think you know me so well, Mr Paras Nath?' She could not help giggling as his ears turned red.

'Call me Paras,' he said gruffly. His name, she could see, was a sore point. Their tête-à-tête would not go unobserved in the constrained environment of their college. Though Paras did not repeat his advice to her, she knew she had to stop caring about what the rest of the world—her college mates or her family—might think about her at every step.

Apparently encouraged by her refusal to rebuff him, Paras came up to her again the next day and suggested they have coffee in the cafeteria. The time to turn him down was now, if she wanted to, because he'd just made it clear he wanted to take their acquaintance to the next level. The longer she delayed her decision, the harder it would become. But she felt in control—he could go ahead only if she let him; she could back out whenever she felt uncomfortable. And she would show Paras and everyone else that she did not give a damn what they thought of her.

'I have come on my bike today,' she said.

'I know. I saw you. And guess what, I got my bike back too.'

'Congrats. What did you do? Fall at your father's feet?'

Paras spluttered with derisive laughter. 'No way! I made him realize how wrong he was.'

'Too bad. If you hadn't got your bike back, I was thinking of offering you a lift to college, instead of Priya.'

'Really? You would? In that case I'll return the keys to my father.'

'You believe anything!' Sulochana laughed. 'So you wouldn't mind sitting behind a girl?'

'Oh, I'd love to sit behind you.'

Emboldened by not seeing any sign of discouragement, Paras proposed they bunk college. Though college was a convenient rendezvous, the hundreds of prying eyes made him uncomfortable. He acted with caution, asking her to ride out first. He would follow on his bike five minutes later. Sulochana doubted whether this subterfuge would fool anybody.

His flattery apart, he did seem different from the others. Instead of merely ogling at her like the rest of his gang, she could see that he was truly impressed by the sight of her on her bike and what it took for her to get on it. At any rate, if he was a chauvinist, he at least bothered to hide it from her. She wished he would stop being part of that bunch of losers so that she could stop comparing him with them at every step. The first thing she would do would be to get him a good haircut.

Away from college and riding alongside Paras, Sulochana felt an air of liberation. Riding the SZ now came so naturally to her that she laughed recalling the initial days when she could barely budge the bike from its place. Now she could zip past Paras, leaving him astounded. 'Give me that bike,' Paras said, 'and I'll spin circles around you.' She laughed him off, revved up the accelerator and whizzed ahead before slowing down to let him catch up with her. The rides were exciting but ended where Bisalpur ended, all too soon. Neither of them wanted to sail down the national highway just yet.

So, on Paras's insistence, they turned back and stopped at the classiest restaurant in town—Bisalpur Palace. It was the default venue for any well-to-do citizen of Bisalpur who wanted to host a party, or a wedding reception. Sulochana had never been inside before, and Paras's only visit had been courtesy Gajanan's birthday party a year back. Feeling out of place suddenly in its dimly lit interiors with soft music playing in the background, and taken aback by the blast of the air-conditioning, Sulochana said, 'Paras, let's go. It'll be too expensive here. You don't have to do this.'

Paras dismissed her suggestion but she saw him wince looking at the menu. After they'd ordered a cold coffee and a brownie with hot chocolate each, Paras told her she could make herself look more like Komal by altering her hairstyle.

'I don't want to be Komal. I want to be me.'

'Yes, yes, of course, I didn't mean that. I meant you can look a lot more stylish, and beautiful, if you try.'

'You mean I look ugly now?'

'No, what are you saying?' Paras began protesting in earnest, before realizing she was pulling his leg. 'Why are you ragging me? I am your senior, you know.'

He was her senior, but only in years. Otherwise, she was the one who felt in control, who could make him laugh or fall into despair. What was the point of exerting influence over him? Like their bike journeys on the roads of Bisalpur, her joy would be short-lived. What after that? Suddenly, the ambience of Bisalpur Palace seemed oppressive.

'Let's leave, Paras.'

'Why? What happened? It's so cool in here. Let's enjoy ourselves a little longer now that that we have shelled out so much.'

'What do you want, Paras?'

'What do I want? Nothing, really. I don't understand. Just spending time with you like this.'

He was making it all even more oppressive.

'Let's be honest with each other. You like me,' she said flatly.

His jaw dropped. 'Y... yes. And you? Do you like me too?'

'It depends.'

'On what?'

She sighed. She would have to spell it out for him. It was unfair of her to expect him to understand what she wanted. 'You are a good guy, Paras. But that's not enough for me. My liking you depends on what you want, on what you want to achieve in life.'

His baffled expression revealed that he obviously did not have a clue about what she meant, or what she was getting at.

'Do you want to stay in Bisalpur all your life, Paras? Or do you want to get out?'

His brow cleared. 'Out, of course. No way can I live here all my life like my father.'

'And live your own life, outside? On your own terms, no one to ask questions, and no one to answer to?'

'Yes, exactly like that. But how?'

She had to laugh at his naiveté. 'Look, don't just say yes because I am asking you. Tell me honestly, do you want to make it big outside or not? Forget the how, but do you want to? Don't lie to me, please. I'll know if you are speaking the truth or not.'

He looked at her as if judging whether she was pulling his leg again, but not finding any trace of humour in her expression, decided that she was indeed serious, and put on a grave face himself. 'Yes, I want to make it big. To be honest, I have not given much thought on how to how to go about it. But I feel suffocated here. Is it...is it that important to you, getting out of here?'

She nodded, not trusting herself to speak without bursting into tears. Paras slowly reached out and took her hand. She did not withdraw, surprised at the thrill of his touch. Paras looked at their joined hands on the table, as though taking his gaze away from them might make his dream vanish in a puff of smoke.

'So you like me?' he asked.

'No, I only let people I don't like hold my hand after going with them to a restaurant. And now let go, because that waiter is staring at us.'

'We won't be able to escape stares in Bisalpur, Sulo.'

'I know. That's what I don't like about this place.'

'I believe we are meant for each other,' he said in a hoarse whisper. 'Do you care very much what others think?'

That was a gauntlet she had to pick up. 'No, I don't,' she said squeezing Paras's hand and staring back at the waiter.

The passing rate in the Political Science course at Residency College, Bisalpur, seldom fell below 100 per cent. The reason behind this impressive statistic was not the academic brilliance of its pupils but the graciousness shown by its lecturers whilst correcting the examination papers. Failing a student almost always got the parents involved. Having to coexist in the same town with aggrieved parents and knowing that in the long-term scheme of things, it hardly mattered whether Subhadra Kumari scored 32 per cent (fail) or 38 per cent (pass), the lecturers were prone to awarding a few grace marks here and there if they nudged a student across the threshold.

Two failures then, in the same class, was a remarkable achievement because it meant the examiner had decided that even grace marks would not suffice. Sulochana was mortified to learn that she was one of the two to achieve this distinction. Soon, however, her mortification turned to bemusement. How had *she* managed to fail a course when no one else had for the past three years?

Having to take the examinations again next year would be a bother, but apart from the inconvenience and paperwork, it did not matter. With the kind of reputation Bisalpur Residency had, jobs were not going to fall into her lap even if she topped her batch. So she stopped grieving over her failure quickly and forgot to hide her marksheet at home. That her mother would come across it, scrutinize it and draw conclusions, did not even strike her.

'Sulochana? What's this? 22 out of 100? "F"? Does it mean you failed in this subject?'

Sulochana tried hard to find something to divert her mother's attention, but in vain; the evidence against her was too incriminating. 'Yes, Mamma, but it's not an important subject. I don't know what went wrong. These lecturers give marks without even looking at the paper. They give marks to their favourite students who flatter them. I don't do all that. I—'

'How can you fail?' her mother said, almost screaming.

'I said, it's not that important. Another girl failed too.'

'It's important for you because you said you wanted to be a lecturer. How can you become a lecturer if you fail? What will you teach others if you fail yourself?'

The irrefutability of her mother's argument stunned Sulochana into silence. She could not deny that she was the one who had insisted she wanted to become a lecturer when her uncle and her mother were discussing her future after her father's death. But couldn't they see she had simply blurted out the first thing that came to mind because she was scared they were thinking of marrying her off at the age of nineteen or twenty? They were adults who were supposed to understand her, so why couldn't they see through her lies when she said she wanted to study, become a lecturer and stand on her own feet? The last point had won her mother over, who after her husband's death, could not undermine the importance of a woman's financial independence.

So flunking her subject had considerably weakened her side of the case.

'Listen, Sulo,' her mother continued, 'I believed you then despite your uncle's opposition. You have to concentrate on your studies.'

'I do, Mamma. Something has gone wrong with the paper correction. I'll find out and apply for re-evaluation. It happens every year.'

As though she had not even spoken, or whatever she said was irrelevant, her mother carried on from where she had paused, much to Sulochana's annoyance. 'I let you ride the bike to college, wearing those modern clothes. I don't like it, but I let you go like that because you want to be independent and free.'

'Mamma—'

'Wanting to be independent and free requires courage and you have that, I grant you. You want to have the good things that come with being free, that I can understand. But then you also have to stand on your own feet. That's when you'll really be free because no one can question you.'

'This is just one subject. Don't talk as if it is the end of the world!'

It seemed as if her words bounced off a glass wall, for all the effect they had on her mother. 'You do not live in a millionaire's family, understand? What you want to achieve, you do on your own. Otherwise, shut up, keep out of the limelight and get married to someone who will entertain your dreams.'

'How did we start talking about my marriage? I just don't understand you sometimes.'

'I am trying to get through to you myself! Please understand one simple fact—you cannot enjoy the fruits of freedom without having earned that freedom. Heed my experience in life.'

'What experience, Mamma?' asked Sulochana sarcastically. 'You have hardly been out of the house alone, other than going to the bhaji market.'

'That's true. I don't go out with some guy on a bike, like you.'

Had her mother jabbed her in the abdomen, she could not have been more effective in taking the wind out of her.

Sulochana could only stare at her mother. 'This is Bisalpur,' her mother said quietly. 'You think no one will see you?'

'I am sick of this place and the people. They put two and two together and make 222—it's none of their business, I've done nothing wrong,' Sulochana said, feeling her mouth turn sour with anger. She went across to her room to put an end to the conversation, but her mother followed her.

'I just want you to be careful so that you don't end up neither here nor there. If you want freedom, you work for it. Otherwise, live like the rest of us. And why are your clothes lying like this on the bed? Can't you take care of your own room, if not the house?'

Under normal circumstances, Sulochana would be irked no end by her mother's harrying her about the upkeep, or the lack of it, of her room. But now, she was relieved that her unsorted clothes had diverted her mother's mind from the subject of her future. 'Learn some household work, Sulochana,' her mother said, folding her clothes and stacking them in sorted heaps in the wardrobe. 'You need to—what's this?'

Her mother was holding a bright scarlet lacy brassiere by her fingertips at arm's length, as though bringing it any closer would contaminate her. Along with the tank top and short skirt, it was one of Sulochana's prized possessions, kept carefully concealed in the secret inner recess of the wardrobe. She must have tried it on and preened before the mirror, but forgotten to return it to its hiding place.

'My bra, of course,' she said, brazening it out. 'What's there to ask?'

'I know that, but why...why this bright red, this fancy stuff? Aren't the normal white ones I get good enough for you?'

Sulochana rolled her eyes heavenwards to beseech the gods. 'White is so boring.'

'Boring? What can be interesting or boring in a bra?'

'Why are we even discussing what bra I wear?'

'How much did it cost?'

'Four hundred,' she said, and immediately regretted blurting out the true price.

'Four hundred! Are you mad? I could get you half a dozen normal ones for that much. How can you spend so much on a bra?'

'It's worth it. It looks good.'

'Looks good?' Her mother was echoing everything she said. 'Looks good to whom? Who is going to see it? Who is going to see it, tell me? Are you going to walk out in that?'

'Looks good to me. I feel good about it, that's all,' she retorted.

Her mother could not fathom her defiance. 'I am warning you, Sulochana. I don't know what path you are going on, but it is wrong. Think about your sister.'

'What about her? She will do what she feels is right, not what I do. I don't ask anyone to follow me or imitate me, just leave me alone. And, wearing a red bra does not mean going down a wrong path.'

'You are talking like this because I am alone,' said her mother in an injured tone. 'If your father was here, you wouldn't behave like this. I—'

'Stop!'

Her father knew how to live; how to be happy without feeling guilty over it. He would simply have laughed her mother's worries off. She could never fathom how he and her mother had gotten along.

'If he were here, I would not have to hide everything I like. Leave my father out of this, please.'

Sulochana now understood what Paras meant when he said you ran out of options in Bisalpur so quickly. In a city like Delhi you would not have to rack your brains about where to go with your boyfriend or girlfriend. Scores of multiplexes, shopping malls and arcades, restaurants or fast-food joints, or all of them together in one place, parks and gardens—there was no dearth of choices. If nothing else, you could simply lose yourself in the crowd.

Bisalpur had one of each—one multiplex, one shopping mall, one public garden and one decent restaurant—as though it was necessary to possess at least one to qualify as a city. The restaurant they had already been to several times already, despite its distinctly unBisalpur-like prices. The garden was kept locked most of the day, with only the gardeners tending to it, enjoying their siesta inside it. It opened early morning to let in elderly walkers and strollers, and in the evening, when bunches of kids scampering all over demolished any potential for privacy and romance. Only the sole multiplex—comprising two screens—had an ambience where a guy and a girl could be seen together without inviting scandalized looks.

Initially, they rode their own bikes, with Sulochana now and then using her more powerful engine to race ahead of Paras and annoy him, or cutting him too close while overtaking him so that he was forced to brake. 'Sulo, cut the stunts!' But they quickly realized that this way of travelling was not only a waste of petrol and precious pocket money, it also kept them unnecessarily apart. If word was getting around that they were gallivanting together, it didn't matter whether they went on one bike or were careful about showing that they kept their distance, because the rumour-mongers would tell the tale the way they wanted to anyway.

So they began using one bike, either hers or Paras's. Sometimes, Paras sat behind but usually he was the one riding the bike, glad that for once he was able to get the feel of a powerful machine. And his sitting pillion behind her attracted more glances than if they sat the other way round.

Their only private moments were shared inside the movie hall, after the movie began and the lights were switched off. The best shows, meaning the ones with scant attendance, were the early matinee ones on weekdays, which meant bunking college, and which both were able to do without much compunction. English movies rarely came to Bisalpur, but if they did, they proved to be good shows from the couple's perspective, almost guaranteed to have a limited audience. Besides, neither of them spoke or understood too much of the language anyway.

Another precaution they adopted, but soon dispensed with, was of Paras going alone to buy the tickets and Sulochana joining him in the hall a few minutes later. The best-placed seats, they found, were at the back in the corner of the last row, but they were also the ones that cost the most. The ushers were trained to ensure that no one from the cheaper seats moved to the expensive ones, if they were unoccupied.

The jaunts to the restaurant and the movies brought Paras perilously close to being broke, until one day he was forced to admit it. 'Sorry, Sulo, I just don't get enough pocket money. My father...'

She had been waiting for that confession. 'Guys and their egos! I know you have a problem, but why hide it? I am not well-off either, but we can pool in our money, whatever we have, okay?'

'You are the best, Sulochana,' said Paras, beaming so hard that she knew he meant it.

It was only inside the movie hall, cloaked in the darkness, shielded from real and imaginary prying eyes, that they could be themselves. She stifled her giggles as his hands wandered over her arms and legs. She sensed his hesitation as his hand hovered over her shoulder and withdrew. Towards the end of the movie, he must have grown desperate. He grabbed her face and locked his mouth over hers, making her incapable of even gasping in surprise, or shock, or anger. Then, the moment to react passed and she decided she rather liked the sensation of his rough mouth on her lips, the slobberiness and wetness of his lips and tongue.

Just as she was slipping into a dreamy state, she realized his hand was cupping her breast. She pushed him away violently. 'That's too much.'

'What? Okay, look, sorry, I got carried away. I won't do that, okay?'

'Don't act innocent now.'

'I said I am sorry. It's just that we never get time to be alone. We are always hiding from something or someone.'

'Paras, listen,' she whispered. 'Kissing and stuff is fine, but I know that you...oh all right, both of us will not want to stop at that. But that's not possible here in Bisalpur.'

'Sulo, I love you.'

'I love you too, Paras, but that's not the point. People notice if we as much as look at each other. Going further is impossible.'

'But I really believe we are meant for each other. We are soulmates.'

'Yes, and I really believe that you have true feelings for me,' she said, though a little amused to hear him spout lines out of a Shah Rukh Khan movie of the '90s. 'But we don't have a future here.'

'What!!' Paras whispered.

'We have talked about this before. We can think of a life together only if we get out of Bisalpur. You have to get out of here, and help me get out of here, too. That has to be your objective.'

'It is. I haven't forgotten.'

The movie on the screen rolled on unnoticed. At this point, Sulochana did not even bother whether it was an English or a Hindi film.

'Then do something about it. Don't say it just to please me.'

'And if I do, then?'

'Then you get to kiss me and do everything else you have been dreaming about. But not here in Bisalpur.'

CHAPTER 5

Not a day passed without Paras fearing that the heavy hand of some moral authority would fall on his shoulder for going out with Sulochana. But when a month went by without anyone pulling him up for his supposed transgressions, he began wondering if contrary to his assessment, Bisalpur was indeed progressing with the times. Their trysts were no secret in college. Though it made him the target of innuendo-laden jokes, he knew they were laced with an undercurrent of envy and grudging admiration of his success.

To fancy a girl, to muster the courage to go ahead and tell her the same, was not uncommon, but to get one's feelings reciprocated was a rare instance in the annals of Bisalpur Residency College.

Priya caught on soon enough by tapping into the rumour mills and finding both her brother and Sulochana missing from college every afternoon. The clincher lay in their half-hearted denials. Paras had snapped at her when she asked. 'Yes, we are going out. What's that to you? Are you trying to take Papa's place?'

'I am not,' she said. 'Remember, it was because of me that you met her. I can be of help, you know, if and when required.'

Paras thanked her and said the greatest help would be to keep quiet about it at home, so that the parents would not suspect anything. Priya kept her word but their precautions were in vain. Paras's father came to know of his exploits through another source and stopped him just as he was about to slip into his room.

'Where are you coming from, Paras?'

His tone made it clear that matters were about to come to a head again.

'Just out with friends. Like every day,' replied Paras.

'Enough of that!' His father's explosion caught Paras by surprise, by its sheer volume. 'Stop thinking that you are the cleverest person in the world and that the rest of us are fools. You go roaming with girls to movies on my bike, which I gave you so that you don't waste time going to and from college. Instead,' he said, turning to his wife, 'our son thinks he is a film star like...like Rishi Kapoor.'

Paras tried hard to suppress his laughter, turned away and, catching Priya's glance, couldn't hold back a snort.

'What are you laughing at, fool?'

'Rishi Kapoor is so old. His son Ranbir is the hero nowadays.'

His father glared at him with the intensity of an oxy-acetylene torch. 'As long as you drive my bike, and spend my money, you will not disobey me. The pocket money I give you is not for spending on girls. It's so that you live a comfortable life, so that you can focus on your studies. Am I clear?'

Paras pretended to listen, striking his usual pseudo-repentant pose—gazing at the ground with bowed head. Some busybody colleague of his father, or a nosy-parker neighbour must have seen him with Sulochana and dutifully reported it to his father. Bisalpuris, frustrated with their own miserable lives, could not stomach the happiness of others.

'You don't know how fortunate you are,' his father said, harking back to his favourite subject—that of Paras's good fortune and his disappointing blindness in not recognizing it, 'to get a bike and pocket money of your own. Do you think I got a fraction of all that from my father, who had five sons and two daughters to look after?'

'Of my own, you said,' Paras replied. 'Then let me spend it where I want to, and how I want to. I am not stealing or robbing or buying drugs with that, right? If you are giving me the money and bike for my own use, then don't impose conditions on it. I fill the petrol from my pocket money. I don't ask you to give me a separate amount for the petrol.'

'I am so grateful for that. You know what, it is *my* hard-earned money and so I *will* impose conditions on how you spend it. You will spend it for productive purposes, and not on girls. You are not old enough for that. If you don't like my conditions, don't take the money.'

'Then don't say it is money of my own. And I am old enough, I will be twenty-one in two months.'

'You will be old enough when you start earning and become independent. Until then you are not.'

'Oh, it's always money, money, money. I'll show you.'

'Please do. Why do I get the feeling I have heard all this before?'

Paras stormed out of the house, slamming the door behind him, convinced he would say or do something terrible if he continued sparring with his father, and yet overwhelmingly aware of his impotence. He wished he had at least broken a thing or two to register his anger.

He walked swiftly, almost at a jog, for a few minutes, enveloped in a cloud of fury. Slowly, when the adrenaline fell to more reasonable levels, he breathed easier as he realized he had put in quite some distance from his house. Just the act of getting away from the claustrophobic atmosphere of home made him feel that much lighter. How much better would he feel, he couldn't help thinking, if he was out of Bisalpur itself?

Sulochana's instinctive belief that their escape from the confines of Bisalpur was the key to their happiness was correct. The girl was to be admired. When she had put forward that condition the first time, he had been taken aback but had agreed because what other option did he have? He would have happily walked on one foot for a year if that was what she wanted from him. At that time, he had mentally dismissed her condition as a temporary whim—a fanciful notion that only a girl could come up with. But now, he realized that she could see the big picture which insight he had then lacked.

At the time he had thought her hard-nosed but the reality of her statement, that they had no future together in Bisalpur, was undeniable. Once outside, in some big city like Delhi or Mumbai, he was confident she would give in to him. Her practical attitude was probably just a mask that would fall away as soon as she was beyond the claustrophobic reach of Bisalpur. And it would not hurt him to thumb his nose at his father by being independent.

He, along with Sulochana, had to get out; it was no more a question of why, but of how.

He had not stolen a rupee, but in his father's eyes, he was no better than a petty criminal. If you went by the newspaper stories, there were youngsters his age who bashed in their parents' heads for money. But for his father, his being seen with a girl was enough to bring the heavens down. In the cities having a girlfriend was something to be flaunted, not just in front of your friends, but even in front of your parents. Not only was it accepted, it was expected.

His father surely must have caught a glimpse of those reality shows on TV while surfing the channels. Didn't it ever strike him then, watching those guys and girls on bikes in *The Real Deal*, or in the other one that had couples forming and splitting all the time, that they were a part of the same society he was in? All those boys and girls had parents somewhere, in big cities or small towns, some of whom were probably not even aware of what their children did. Of those who were aware, some probably switched off their TV sets, disgusted by the sight of their daughter frolicking with some unknown guy in a swimming pool, while others basked in the reflected glory of the few episodes of fame their child was bringing them. Did his father ever stop to ponder all that or did he simply brush it aside with a dismissive shake of his head because it was too far outside his experience, too unreal for him to weigh in his mind?

Paras stopped short suddenly, as though he had run into a wall. Why hadn't it struck him before? Now he would have to wait until the next day to share his brainwave with Sulochana because it was too late in the evening for them to meet, and not something that could be discussed casually over the phone. Damn Bisalpur!

He expected Sulochana to be surprised when he sounded her out the next day, but not to the extent of staring at him open-mouthed, as if he had just suggested that they elope at once and get married in a temple. 'Are you out of your mind, Paras?'

'Hello!? You were the one goading me to get out of Bisalpur, and now when I suggest a way, you think I am crazy!'

'Yes, but it has to be practical, not your fantasy. Join *The Real Deal*, indeed! They are just waiting for us with garlands to welcome us on the show.'

'All right, forget I said that,' Paras said, tiring of her sarcasm. 'Let's both study hard, top the college, get gold medals and get the best paying jobs in Delhi.'

Sulochana held her stomach, laughing. 'We have a better chance of winning *The Real Deal* than we have of topping.'

'Or,' Paras continued, 'I could go to Mumbai and try becoming a hero there. With my wonderful looks, body, acting ability and connections in Bollywood, that should be very easy for me. Once I become successful, I will make you my heroine. How about that?'

'Stop already. Not funny.'

'Then the most practical and realistic thing to do is to do absolutely nothing. Let everything carry on the way it is, and we can stay put in Bisalpur all our lives.'

She must have realized that her barbs had hurt him, so she hastened to mollify him. 'Mr Paras Nath is angry. I am sorry. But Paras, the idea of participating in *The Real Deal* is so…so… what can I say?'

'Ridiculous? Look, I know it sounds that way but we have to try, Sulo, because there is no other option if we want to make it big. That's what you mean by getting out of Bisalpur, right?'

Sulochana nodded glumly.

'Then *The Real Deal* is the only place where it's possible to make it big without already being a celebrity, without being stinking rich, without having to be brilliant at academics or sports or singing or acting or looking like a supermodel. We have to be smart and play it right. That's the only talent we'll need.'

That little speech of his had the effect of shutting her up momentarily. He could see she was impressed by the amount of thought he had invested. When she spoke again, her voice was devoid of the acerbity it had contained earlier. 'That's true, but how do we get in? How do we qualify? And even if we do, how do we stay in and not get voted out right at the beginning? Everyone else would be from big metros and we from Bisalpur... We just can't compete.'

'And,' Paras added, 'you are assuming both of us will qualify together.'

'Hah! Right. See? You yourself are picking holes in your idea.'

'All right. So the alternative is to drop the idea and do nothing. That should work.'

'No!' Sulochana said vehemently. 'That's not what I meant. I appreciate your thinking about getting out of here and acting on it. Let us identify the problems and figure out the solutions. We should sit down and think clearly about what to do. Unless we try, we'll never know.'

'That's my girl! That's the Sulo I know,' Paras said. 'That's what I expect from you. Now let's put our heads together.'

To show Sulochana his sincerity and diligence, Paras came prepared with a carefully thought-out list the next day, and was pleased to find that Sulochana was ready with her own laundry list. On comparing notes, they found seven items common to both lists. Their final list contained the following:

1) non-metro background;
2) poor English;
3) no money;
4) clothes (only on Sulochana's list);
5) parents'/family's approval
6) good physique, lack of (only on Paras's list);
7) playing the game, if selected;
8) hairstyle (only on Sulochana's list);
9) how to qualify in interviews and auditions; and
10) both from the same place—Bisalpur.

'That's all?' Paras asked, going over the collated list. 'Can you think of anything else?'

'That's all? This is twice more than enough. How many more problems do you want?'

'I would rather know about them now than discover new ones at the last moment when it could be too late to do anything.'

'It is already too late to do anything.'

'Come on, Sulo!' Paras was stung by her moroseness. 'Don't give me that loser talk again. We will never get anywhere if we think that way. We have time on our side. We can prepare for a year and try to qualify next year.'

'Next year?'

'Yes, I believe that's the best way,' Paras said, finding his own idea more convincing now that he dwelt on it. 'Let's first get rid of the minor problems, or those that we can't do much about, and then let's focus on a plan for the major ones.' He could not help noticing that in spite of her objections, Sulochana was showing some kind of deference to his opinions, a novel and gratifying experience for him.

The easiest items to tick off the list were 'clothes' and 'hairstyle'. Both agreed that given a reasonable amount to spend, Sulochana could make a vast improvement in those areas without much effort. Even Bisalpur possessed one or two good hairdressers and boutiques usually patronized by the Bisalpur elite, which ought to serve the purpose.

But the condition they assumed as 'given' led directly to the seemingly insurmountable and unavoidable problem #3, 'no money'. Paras and Sulochana stared at each other, hoping that one of them would come up with a magical solution. Finally, Paras said, 'I guess we need to save, and then pool in our pocket money.' But even as he said it, he knew it was not good enough.

Sulochana's expression told him that she thought likewise. 'How much can we save? Our pocket money doesn't exactly run into lakhs.'

Paras shrugged. 'Then we have to ask our parents.'

'Fine sense of humour, I see. You seriously think they will give us a paisa to spend on clothes and hairstyle and stuff?'

'Short of robbing someone, or winning a lottery, this is the only practical way left. We will have to convince them to give us a chance. It's not that we will need an unlimited amount. Once we get into the show, the channel will take care of all the expenses. They take away your cash and cards, in fact, so that you don't have anything to spend.'

'How do you know all this?'

'Oh, you find things out when you want to. I have done my homework.'

Sulochana was impressed. 'Maybe I should start paying more attention to what you say! I know for sure Mamma will say no.'

'I am sure you have a better chance with your mother than I have with my father. You can try emotionally blackmailing her. My father will get a heart attack laughing if I go that route.'

Shaking her head, Sulochana made sad little asterisks against a few items on the list. 'Nothing we can do about these. Non-metro background, poor English, your physique and both of us being from Bisalpur.'

'What's wrong with my physique?'

'You tell me, you put it on the list,' Sulochana said.

'Make it better. Bulk up a bit, look toned, get six-pack abs.'

'Get real. Do some exercises and look fit, that's enough. You can't become Hrithik Roshan in a few months.'

She must have seen his face fall because she said immediately, 'I like you how you are; you are good enough for me. I don't like Hrithik that much anyway.'

Both agreed that they could not alter the fact of growing up in a small town. 'But,' Paras said, 'we can do something about both of us being from Bisalpur.'

'How so? And actually, what's wrong in coming from the same place?'

'Okay, imagine for a moment we both do well in the qualifying rounds. But one of us is almost guaranteed to be rejected. Two or three selections from a big metro like Delhi is fine, but not two from Bisalpur. They want variety in the contestants on the show. You have to show you come from somewhere else, and that we don't even know of each other's existence.'

Sulochana frowned in concentration and then suddenly snapped her fingers. 'I was in Mirauli until class five. My uncle still lives there. I can give his address as mine.'

'There you go. We just happen to be from nearby towns and have nothing to do with each other. That's very important.'

She nodded, but he could see she was having her doubts about the whole affair.

'Look, Sulo, being from a small place has its advantages because those people want a variety on the show. If everyone is from Delhi or Mumbai, it becomes boring. So they always select two or three people from the small towns. We have a chance of getting selected because we are non-metro, but once in, we have to play smart, and not stand out.'

'If we have time, we can improve,' she said. 'We can join spoken English and personality development courses. I have seen an institute on Mall Road offering them.'

Paras squeezed her hand in delight. 'That's the way to go about it. It's great we think together. I am sure your mother will not disapprove of spending on educational causes.'

'Yes, but how do we get shortlisted, and how do we handle the personal interviews?'

'Slow down,' Paras said, holding his hand up as though halting traffic. 'I haven't thought of everything. Today is just the first day. We will have to come up with a proper plan.'

A few moments later: 'Paras? What style do you think will suit me, long or short hair?'

'Shoulder-length. Think of Komal. Model yourself on her. Beautiful girl who can also handle a big bike. That's a killer combo.'

'Really? You think I can be like that?'

'Of course, Sulo.' It was interesting. The more he took charge, the more confident of himself he sounded, the more she sought his approval. 'Those city girls look hep just because of their make-up and clothes. But truly speaking, you are more beautiful than most of them.'

'Most.'

'All of them,' Paras corrected himself quickly. 'What's funny?'

'Nothing. Just imagining Mamma's face the day she sees me in my new avatar.'

CHAPTER 6

Getting used to the hardships caused by their self-imposed austerity turned into severe tests of self-control. Paras, if he could help it, tagged along with Priya in a cycle-rickshaw. Sulochana refrained from purchasing any new perfumes or lipsticks or trinkets that caught her fancy. Their frequent trips to the matinee shows were severely curtailed, as were the cold coffees and ice creams at Bisalpur Palace. The sole reason they could not totally stop going there was that it was just about the only place where they could sit in comfort and have some semblance of privacy while talking. The price for that was at least one coffee or milkshake and a moderately generous tip before they left.

By the time they became inured to their penury over the course of several weeks, they had enough cash in hand for Sulochana to go to Lucy's Hairstylists (Ladies Only)—Bisalpur's Finest, and for Paras to enrol in the six-month membership programme at the Atlas gym, and to enquire about the possibility of discounted rates for students at the Excel Institute for the spoken English and personality development courses.

At the end of the three-hour long session at the hairstylists', Sulochana was relieved that she had had the foresight to carry more cash than what she had anticipated she would need. She received the bill of Rs 1,100 with a mixed bag of emotions—crying out at the extravagance, but satisfied that the result was worth it.

As she surveyed her infinite reflections in the array of mirrors to her front, back and the sides, she thought of Paras, and then found herself shaking her head with a smile. She could not have imagined a few weeks ago that she would become so dependent on him for his approval. To be fair to Paras, he had earned the right to be considered dependable.

Ever since he had thrown himself headlong into the preparation for *The Real Deal*, not for one moment had he let her slack, or allowed her to doubt herself. It was as though it was originally his idea to escape Bisalpur. His enthusiasm so surpassed her own that she was almost relieved to let him take over the reins.

Because with him, as always, she felt she was the one in control. If he took charge of *The Real Deal* campaign, it was only because she let him. Even when they French-kissed in the gloomy secrecy of the cinema halls, or held hands in open view of the Bisalpur Palace clientele, the comforting thought at the back of her mind was that whatever was happening was because she willed it so. If she did not want it to happen, it would not. Paras, to his credit, did not try to be greedy and disturb the equilibrium of their relationship. And of late, she realized she had stopped thinking about who the one in control was because she was happy being with him and the rest did not matter.

She trusted him because she knew he had her best interests in mind. He was right in predicting what a magical transformation a few crisp notes of currency could accomplish.

The hairstylist had thrown in a mini-facial as part of the package. Her face glowed; her skin was smooth and soft as a baby's; her eyebrows shaped such that not a hair marred their perfect symmetry.

But what made her almost unrecognizable from her old self was her altered hairstyle. Her hair now reached a point barely a finger-length below her shoulders, the ends forming a shallow 'U', while giving an impression of being subtly waved at the sides.

Paras's reaction to her new look would tell her whether the experiment had been a success. He would be waiting outside to pick her up. She could not imagine putting on a helmet and crushing her hair now; she would have to figure out some way to get around that—tie a scarf, maybe. Without some protection, the wind would play havoc with her hair and she would end up looking more like a scary witch than a breathtaking beauty.

Certainly, breathlessness was one of the major symptoms Paras displayed on seeing her. 'Wow! I knew it, I knew it!' was all his excitement would allow him to exclaim for a few seconds. 'Look at you, Sulo, you are so beautiful. They will die to get you on the show.'

'Really? You think so?' Sulochana asked, basking in pleasure.

'I think? I can certify it. You are better than Komal.'

'Wow. That is the ultimate compliment from you.'

'No, I mean it,' Paras said. 'I admit I had my doubts earlier whether my idea was indeed the stupidest and craziest thing one could come up with. But looking at you now, all my doubts are gone. You just tell them that biking is your hobby, and your entry into *The Real Deal* is a cakewalk.'

Sulochana took a quick look around, and finding no one paying attention to them, stepped up to him and pecked him on his cheek. Paras was astounded. 'But—'

'I know, I know, I said no public display of affection. But I was happy and wanted to thank you. Do you mind?' she asked unnecessarily, since his expression made it clear that being kissed by a pretty girl on a public road was the last thing he minded.

At home, the reaction her new look evoked was beyond breathtaking—it sucked the very air out of the lungs of her mother and sister, leaving them dumbstruck. Sulakshana found her tongue first. 'I was going to ask who you were, Didi, when you entered the house! What a lovely cut! Where did you get it?'

'Lucy's, Mall Road,' Sulochana said, keeping an eye on her mother who, strangely, had not interrupted the proceedings with any question of her own.

'Lucy's! Wow. How much did that cost?' Sulakshana asked, excited. 'I will get my hair cut there too.'

'Shut up. First come out of school.'

'Why?' The first salvo fired by her mother was monosyllabic. 'I want to know why you are doing this to me, Sulochana.'

Sulochana let out a deep sigh. It seemed to her that sighing and shrugging and shaking of heads constituted a large portion of the conversation with her mother. 'I am not doing anything to you, Mamma. I did something to myself. I got my hair cut, not yours. See?' she asked, running a hand through her hair.

'Where have I gone wrong?'

She felt a scream well up in her throat. 'Not again! Let me

have my little pleasures, Mamma, when I am young. I won't do or enjoy these things when I am forty. Harmless things that do not hurt or bother anyone else. I saved from the pocket money you let me have, and used it.'

'True, you have done no wrong,' her mother said, outsighing her. 'It's I who have gone wrong somewhere in raising you.'

'I am sick of this!' Sulochana exploded. 'You can't move a finger here without your morals being questioned. Every day the same old circus, the same old frustrating argument. Just get me a purdah and I will sit at home wearing that. Why send me to college?'

Her fierce reaction put the lid on her mother's quest for answers. Sulakshana had withdrawn quietly to her room, deeming it wiser not to get caught in the crossfire. Sulochana felt relieved that she had put an end to the matter so quickly, but also bad at shouting at her mother. But why then did she have to make her struggle for every little bit? In her mother's eyes, anything that made you happy was morally questionable. Being sad and disappointed with your lot, but not doing anything to improve it—was that how you were supposed to live your life? Why were they all so afraid of being happy? The world around them would change, fall to pieces and regenerate anew, but they—her mother, and Bisalpur itself—would shut their eyes and pretend to notice nothing.

God, she missed her father the most at times like these. He would always indulge her and shield her from his wife's homilies, be it the matter of bikes or clothes or make-up.

Perhaps her mother would react positively if she told her about her intention to enrol in the spoken English and personality development classes. Surely, that ought to sound academically inclined to her, and thus something to be encouraged.

Within a couple of days, however, Sulochana realized she had underestimated her mother; far from closing the subject, she had escalated the issue. When she returned home from college, and a meeting with Paras, after both of them had finally managed to convince the manager of Excel Institute to grant them a 40 per cent discount as college students, with the promise that their recommendation would bring in their friends too, she found a visitor awaiting her.

She had never had a favourable impression of her uncle. The only interactions she remembered was of him pulling her cheeks perfunctorily when she was a kid and giving her a chocolate or two when they met once or twice a year. His family seemed to be the only relations they were on talking terms with, especially after her father's death.

'Mamaji! I didn't know you were coming, or I would have come home earlier.'

'Oh, don't worry. Your mother tells me you are very busy these days. We didn't want to disturb your schedule,' he said evenly, eyeing her appearance—the jeans and T-shirt and scarf that she had just untied. 'So how is life, college and your studies?'

So her uncle's appearance was not just a social visit. Her mother must have expressly invited him, and she could bet it had something to do with her new hairstyle and other changes that she had been incorporating into her personality of late. She also realized it was the supercilious look on her uncle's face, which appeared to say—'Whatever you think you know,

I already know about it'—that she had never liked. And today, he simply couldn't wipe that expression off his face.

Her uncle bided his time until dinner was done and the dishes cleared. Then: 'Sulochana, your mother wants you and me to have a talk. To discuss your career and future prospects, you know.'

'Sure,' Sulochana said, partly relieved that matters would be thrashed out and resolved shortly. But dealing with her uncle would require different tactics than those she employed against her mother. Cowing him down with her firmness and stubbornness would not be as straightforward.

'Of course, I wouldn't be talking about all this if your father was here. But unfortunately—and who understands God's wishes—that's how it is, and your mother has entrusted this task to me. Otherwise I would not interfere in your life and your decisions since you are a grown-up now.'

Sulochana nodded, wondering what was coming. She'd found nothing to fault him with, yet. But that was his style. Since her father's death, he had taken up the mantle of guardianship too gravely. She had seen him behave a lot more lightheartedly with his own children, but to her he always showed a sterner side, as though a modicum of levity on his part was not becoming of him as her guardian.

'You had told us last year that you wanted to become a lecturer. But your mother tells me you haven't been doing well in your studies. In fact, you failed in one subject.'

'But Mamaji, the re-evaluation—'

'Let me finish. Then you can tell me your side.' The sudden chill in his voice stopped Sulochana in her tracks. 'If you do badly in your studies, it will become almost impossible to get a lecturership. Are you sure you still want to be a lecturer, or do you want to change your mind, or do you have some other plans?'

'I—'

He held up his hand. Why the heck did he ask her questions when she was not supposed to answer them?

'We want to know what you have in mind because of all the changes—you look so different from the last time I saw you, just a few months ago. Is there anything going on that we ought to know?'

Sulakshana was not around, again tactfully keeping to her room, or perhaps acting on her mother's instructions to keep out of the way. Sulochana could not imagine her uncle welcoming or even hearing out with an open mind her goal of getting into *The Real Deal.* 'No, Mamaji, it's nothing. I just had a haircut. I told Mamma.'

Her uncle looked at her mother and shrugged, as if to say that at least he had tried. 'Well, if you don't have any particular plans, and we don't think that you are really motivated to become a lecturer, what we have decided is that you should get married as soon as you finish your degree.'

Her head reeled. This transition was so abrupt and caught her so unawares that she felt dizzy. 'What? Where did my marriage come up from?'

Her mother spoke now. 'We are not going to pull you out of college to get married, but we will start looking for a suitable boy. You can get engaged and continue in college until you graduate.'

'What suitable boy? I am hardly nineteen, and you want to marry me off!'

'The legal marriageable age is eighteen for women. Your mother got married at the age of seventeen.' Her uncle wrested back the hold on their argument. He had not come this far to play second fiddle. 'And,' he said, barely able to stop smirking, 'it isn't as if you are too young to enjoy the company of boys.'

Sulochana flushed with anger. Uncle or not, he deserved a stinging slap just to wipe away that smirk. How dare he come to their house and talk to her like that! 'If eighteen is the legal age,' she said, finding her voice shaking, 'then I am an adult, and I can do what I please. I don't need your permission.'

'So that's the way of it?' he said, his jaw setting, because he had not expected her to talk back. 'Now I understand what you meant,' he said, turning to her mother. And again, back to her, 'No, you need not glare at your mother. She did what she had to. You have no idea how much hardship she has to face without you giving her more trouble. But get it clear—you cannot frighten me with your rudeness as you do with your mother. Right, so you are an adult; then go and do what you like, but not in this house.'

Was he asking her to leave her own house? And her mother was just standing there, immobile as a statue, without a word in protest?

'Being an adult means not only having rights, but owning up to responsibilities too. I don't hear a word from you now? What happened?'

She detected a sudden tinge of concern in his voice. At the same instant, she also became aware of two things happening, one after the other, a cause and its effect. First, that the strange wet sensation on her cheeks meant she was crying, and second, that the sight of those tears was more effective in checking her uncle's tirade than anything she had spoken. For the first time, she saw him falter, unsure of what to do next. He glanced questioningly at her mother, who was too astonished herself to be of any help.

'All t-this would never happen if my father was here,' Sulochana sobbed.

That made them exchange another doubt-filled glance. 'If he were here,' her mother said, 'matters wouldn't have reached such a stage.'

'Correct. Because he would have let me do what I liked. He would not have forced me to do or not do something.'

'And what is it that you would like to do?' her uncle asked, slowly recovering his poise. 'That's what we want to know. Don't tell me "becoming a lecturer" again!' The sneer was back.

'No, I lied about that then.'

'Aaha. Finally, the truth.'

It was now or never. 'I want to take part in *The Real Deal.*'

'Take part in the what?'

'*The Real Deal.* It's a reality show on TV.'

'On TV?' Flabbergasted, both her uncle and her mother echoed her. Their reaction was comical, but it was no time to become jovial. 'You want to be on a TV show? And they are ready to take you?'

'No, I want to try. It's a competition. You have to qualify for it.'

'Is it that one with motorcycles that you keep watching all the time?' her mother asked. 'And that's why...all this?' She indicated with a sweep of her arms Sulochana's clothes and hair and even the bike outside parked in the veranda.

Sulochana nodded. 'Give me one chance. I want to try for next year's competition. One try, that's all.' She hoped she had injected enough humility into her plea to sway her mother.

'No way. You are not going on TV or anything that enters your mind!'

'Please, Mamma,' Sulochana said, reverting to the teary-eyed and shaky-voiced approach, 'just one chance. If I don't qualify, then I will do whatever you say. Studies or get married, anything you say. Just support me this one time.'

'No means no. On TV, with boys and vulgarity for everyone to see. I won't be able to show my face outside.'

Matters had reached an impasse. She had never seen her mother so obdurate. No amount of impassioned pleading or tears seemed to budge her mother from her stand.

'So you want to try next year?' her uncle asked.

'Yes, Mamaji.' If he was going to follow it up with a smart-alec remark, she would scream at him. They could not expect respect from her if her desires carried so little weight in their minds.

'What are you asking, Brijesh?' her mother asked, angrily. 'It doesn't matter this year or next year because she will not go on any TV show ever.'

'Listen.' He beckoned her mother and told her something so softly that Sulochana could not catch what he said. Her mother drew back, shaking her head, apparently unconvinced.

He turned to Sulochana. 'Are you 100 per cent sure you want to do this? Not some excuse you have just thought of?'

'No! It is the truth this time, I swear.'

'Well, all right,' he said, holding aloft both his hands, telling her to defer her celebration, 'but only on one condition.'

'And you agreed? You agreed?'

'Don't shout, Paras.'

Paras lowered his voice, but his unhappiness was unchanged. 'But how could you, Sulo? Didn't we talk and decide about this very thing? At this very place?'

'That very place' meant their corner table at Bisalpur Palace. They were on a first-name basis with the waiters now.

'What else could I have done?' Sulochana asked, putting on an injured tone. 'If I hadn't agreed, they were bent on getting me married off, forget the show.'

'They must have been bluffing. Who marries at nineteen these days?'

'No, they were not bluffing,' she said, recalling the ordeal. 'Especially my uncle. If I hadn't cried my eyes out and scared them, I would have got nothing.'

'Were you really crying or pretending to?'

'The first tears were real. I felt so sad suddenly, missing my Papa when Mamaji was shouting at me. But when I saw him back off because of my crying, I did a bit of acting too.'

'That's great, Sulo, but, how can we try this year?' His voice rose again as he remembered the reason behind his anguish. 'There's no time to do anything.'

'Some time? Not even a few months?'

'Not more than two months. The application window is already open. Applications will be screened and then the shortlisted ones called for the next round, the interviews. Assuming you qualify, of course.'

'Oh. And that's not enough?' she asked, hardly daring to whisper.

'No! The spoken English and personality development programmes are six-month courses. One year would have given us a chance. That's what we had planned, Sulo.'

'I know, but Mamaji said I could try only once, and it has to be this year. Otherwise nothing doing and get married. Mamma was strictly against this idea too. I don't know how I convinced Mamaji.'

Paras shrugged. 'He probably thought you would do something drastic like running away or hanging yourself if you didn't have your way.'

'Kill myself? Nothing can be so bad to make me want to do that.'

'He doesn't know that. But tell me, why are you so afraid of them? Why do you want their approval?'

Sometimes Paras irritated her. One day he asked her to be practical, and the next he was the one throwing idealism at her. 'If I get their support, I can get more money. We would not have to starve and miss out on all the movies. We could buy good clothes and stuff.'

'That's good, Sulo, but—but it is impossible. Within two months, it is impossible.'

'Why are you talking like a loser now?'

'Because it is impossible, dammit!' He thumped the table hard to reinforce his point, making the cutlery on the table rattle. The waiter frowned at them. They could sit at their table for the price of one coffee as long as they did not bother other customers.

She had wriggled out of one impasse at home but straightaway entered another one with Paras. Even though his hand lay on hers, she could sense him withdraw. Was this suddenly, out of nowhere, the end?

'Well then,' she said, trying to keep her voice even and

dry, 'I suppose I will try this year, and you try the next, or whenever you are ready to. I have to try. My father would have wanted me to.'

'What do you mean?' he asked, coldly.

'I don't see any other way out, Paras.'

'Your father would have encouraged you if he were there?' he asked softly.

She nodded, feeling her tears burgeon again at the mention of her father. 'I think it was his dream, to make me tough, to see me succeed where even most guys can't.'

His grip on her hand tightened until he was hurting her. 'So we will do it for him, Sulo. Together. We both try it this year. I will try to get my family's support.'

'Really, you mean it?'

'Of course. Stop crying now.'

She placed her other hand over his. 'This means so much more to me than when you talk about us being soulmates. That is just talk—fairy tale, filmy stuff. But when you understand what my father meant to me, that is real. I start to believe in soulmates.'

'I couldn't do anything without you,' Paras said, shaking his head. 'Together or nothing.'

'Nor can I,' she whispered. 'I love you, Paras.'

The light that came into his eyes at her words sent a pang through her heart. 'We are always for each other, right, Sulo? Whatever happens, you and I are together.'

'For each other, whatever happens.'

'Promise?'

His innocence touched her. 'Promise. Lifelong.'

The waiter rolled his eyes. 'A Bisalpur Palace special ice cream?' he asked. He knew they could not refuse anything at this moment.

CHAPTER 7

E ven if they had somehow missed noticing the dozens of posters and flyers of *The Real Deal*, the banners of its proud sponsors, the huge makeshift arch welcoming all aspirants, or the scores of volunteers in black *The Real Deal* T-shirts strutting around looking important, Paras and Sulochana would have known that they were at the venue of the Delhi auditions for *The Real Deal* Season 5 just going by the crowd. They had expected a crowd comprising several hundreds, or even a few thousands, but were nevertheless taken aback by the sheer numbers.

The YTV channel, or the organizers they had outsourced the event management to, had arranged for the use of a college ground for holding the auditions over the weekend. Now even that appeared to be as densely crowded as the Kumbh Mela.

Arrow signs on papers stuck to bamboo poles pointed towards various stalls for registration and other activities, trying to create a semblance of order. So did the harried volunteers, trying gamely to shepherd the masses to the appropriate counters in disciplined queues. But the people were just too many; the queues that began kept breaking up and coalescing into confused, impatient and angry bunches.

Paras and Sulochana stood undecided. They had wandered around a few paces soaking in the scene, but were ushered back each time either by the volunteers to join a queue, or by those already in the queue who thought they were trying to jump it. Their anger was justifiable, Paras thought, when he learned that they had been waiting at the venue from 4 a.m. though the counters opened only at 9. And to think he had had misgivings about reaching the place too early, at 8 a.m.!

Perhaps it was better for them to be at the end of the queue, because that gave them more time to get used to the crazy atmosphere. The only time they had encountered crowds like this was during Dussehra at the Ramlila Maidan when people not only from Bisalpur, but also the adjoining villages, poured in to see the forces of good prevail over evil. The crowd was predominantly rustic; in their eyes even Bisalpur was a place to look up to. Paras felt nothing but condescension towards them. Now, he felt—and this was a feeling he could not shake off—that he was at the receiving end of the condescending look. Sulochana and he were the country bumpkins lost in the big city, left desolate even amidst the multitudes. Surely he was not imagining the contemptuous glances those around were throwing at him, or worse—he was the subject of indifference, not even registering on their consciousness. The only reason they even looked in his direction was because Sulochana was with him.

Sulochana herself looked as petrified as him, ignorant of the glances she was attracting. In her expression, in the unseeing stare of her eyes, he could recognize the reflection of his own fear—the fear of being found out. Being identified as an impostor, intruding into places you had no business being in, or trying to be one among people you did not belong to. Bisalpur was stamped all over him; all they needed was one look to figure out his true identity.

Paras had, in fact, already been rejected. He had fallen at the first hurdle—the online shortlisting process. Apparently, his photograph was enough for them to recognize him for what he was; that he did not belong.

The online application process had been straightforward enough—all they had had to do was enter a few standard details from their bio-data, answer a few form questions about why they wanted to enter *The Real Deal*, or what was so different about them that they ought to be a part of *The Real Deal*, upload their photographs and then cross their fingers while waiting for a reply.

Within a few days of the end of the application period, Sulochana had received an email that she had been shortlisted for the New Delhi audition round. She was to present herself in Delhi on 17 May and also on the 18th if she qualified for the actual interview.

Paras, meanwhile, waited in vain for a reply. Only after checking his email account almost once every hour over the next few days did he slowly realize and accept the fact that he had not made it. The other thing he realized was that the selection had more to do with his photograph than his answers, because having filled up the application forms together, there was hardly any variation in their answers. Therefore,

Sulochana's selection and his rejection had to be on the basis of their respective photos—in her new hairstyle, in the most fashionable top she had, in the best photo studio Bisalpur boasted of—the result should have been obvious to him right at the outset.

Sulochana's spontaneous reaction on reading that email was a whoop of joy, and so was Paras's. The email from YTV was an official sanction of their desire. It was the first sign that their dreams would not be limited to building wispy castles in the air, but could also translate into something tangible. Only when Paras said aloud that she had made it, but he had not, was Sulochana's joy muted.

'If you have not made it, Paras, even I won't go,' she said.

'Are you nuts? We have worked so hard for this. You can't let it go now.'

'But we decided we would do everything together.'

'Yes, but all is not lost. I can try again from Chandigarh and Jaipur. I will have a better chance from there. Delhi was always going to be tough.'

'Are you sure?' she asked, now vacillating.

'Of course I am. Now think of how we can go to Delhi together. Will your mother agree?'

'Certainly not if I said I was going with you!'

The queue inched forward. At that rate, it would be a couple of hours before their turn came. They were forced to align themselves in lines in a passageway made out of ropes tied to bamboo poles. Many others joined the queue behind them, so that soon they could see neither the head nor the tail of the queue.

The guy behind Paras tapped him on the shoulder. 'It's all fixed, man. This is my third attempt. But I know they won't select me.'

'Third? But this is the first audition this year.'

'My third year.'

The whole online screening process had been introduced so as to limit the number of aspirants turning up and choking the organizer's resources. The previous year, due to some inevitable delays and confusion, someone had run out of patience and thrown chairs around. Within no time, the disturbance snowballed into a free-for-all mêlée until the police was called in to put an end to the havoc, though by that time almost everything that was not made of metal or not nailed to the ground had been battered or broken or torn apart. The fracas had made for good 'breaking news' clips on the other channels and left *The Real Deal* organizers with red faces and a huge bill.

Going by the numbers milling around the grounds, Paras thought that either most people had simply ignored the results of the online process and still turned up hopeful, or that the screening process had been very liberal (and he was one of the few unlucky ones to have been rejected).

Screams and loud cheers rose from somewhere ahead. Everyone leant over the restraining ropes to find out what the commotion was about. Three people walked alongside the queue, pausing for a few seconds every now and then, and the shouting and jumping followed their progress. When they came a little closer, Paras could make out a man holding a huge video camera, another man with a microphone at the end of a long handle, and a girl with a microphone in her hand that she kept thrusting at the people in the queue.

'Isn't that VJ Shivani?' Sulochana asked.

Paras gasped. VJ Shivani, a former contestant on *The Real Deal*, was one of the most popular VJs on YTV. She had not won *The Real Deal*, but her vivaciousness and kickass attitude had vowed many a viewer. The channel had recognized her popularity and snapped her up immediately after that year's show. And here she was, with tattooed arms and a pierced lower lip, before his eyes, with the mike extended in front of Sulochana's face. 'How do you feel being here? You think you have a chance?'

The question, he was relieved to remember, was not directed at him, because his mind had gone blank. VJ Shivani was no more an apparition on TV, but a real person in flesh and blood; the video camera's unflinching gaze recorded his stupid expression for eternity, and the roar of the crowd around him scared away any coherent thought.

'Good. I am feeling good,' Sulochana said, her voice shaking so badly that Shivani's eyebrows shot up in surprise. 'I don't know if I have—'

The guy behind Paras, who was trying his luck for the third straight year, pushed Paras out of his way and screamed into Shivani's mike. 'I am ready and I am here to win. Everyone, be very afraid because Rajiv is here to kick your ass! Whooo!'

'That's the spirit!' Shivani screamed along with him before moving on.

Paras and Sulochana looked at each other, dumbstruck.

'So that's the way,' Paras said.

'Show that you are confident, that you will win.'

'Even if inside you know you can't, and you are scared.'

'That's the way.' Sulochana smiled, eyes shining with the light of ingrained wisdom. 'But Paras, look at those girls, jabbering away in English. If it wasn't for their English, I would...'

'Forget them. They are all show-offs,' he said with disdain. 'You are better than everyone. I know that.'

'Thank you for believing in me.'

'Let's just get you registered and then think about the next step.'

The queue inched forward, slowly but steadily. It took them a little more than an hour to reach the counters, a bit quicker than he had anticipated. Multiple counters catered to the candidates based on the application numbers that had been allotted when they had submitted the online forms. The girl behind the counter was efficient, looking to dispose of each person as quickly as she could.

'Name? Application number?' She located 'Sulochana Gupta' on the third page. 'ID?'

Sulochana presented her college ID card.

The girl glanced at it for a millisecond, and then tore out a leaflet from another book on which she wrote Sulochana's name and number, a time of 3 p.m. and the location 'Lecture Room-II', and finally affixed the stamp of *The Real Deal* to grant it official status.

'There,' she said. 'It's 3 p.m. In this room. Carry this. This is your entry ticket.'

'To the interview?' Sulochana asked.

'Not so fast. You go through a GD first. If you qualify in that, then you reach the interview stage. Thank you, next please.'

'GD?' Sulochana was aghast.

'Group discussion!' The girl's look made it clear that it was her lot to meet all kinds of people.

'Yes, I know,' Sulochana said, 'but we were not told anything about any group discussion.'

'And how do you think we can interview 2,500 people in two days?'

'What's the GD topic?' Paras asked.

'You will know that on the spot, of course. You cannot prepare for it.' The girl laughed.

'And how many from each group will be selected?'

'I don't know. Someone from the panel will obviously observe the GD and decide. Next please,' she said, losing her smile. 'You are blocking others. I can't keep answering you the whole day.'

Moving away, Sulochana hissed into Paras's ear. 'It's your fault. You didn't prepare me for the GD.'

Reaching Delhi had not been simply a trivial matter of looking up the train timetable and hopping onto the next available train. When the euphoria of the news of Sulochana's selection subsided a notch, her mother was the first to raise the practical question of how she was going to go to Delhi and stay there for a day or two, if required. Once again, she turned to her brother, who gallantly offered his services to escort Sulochana to Delhi, to the competition and back to Bisalpur, though he made a great deal of the leaves of absence he would be forced to avail in order to indulge his niece's whims.

On Paras's instigation, Sulochana protested. 'Come on, Mamma, I can do this alone. I will be on my own in the show, if I am selected. Do you think Mamaji will escort me on the show too?'

'Alone? Is there no end to your craziness? Do you have any idea how dangerous a city like Delhi is for young single girls?'

Paras felt like tearing out clumps of hair from someone's head, if not his own. Were they to be stymied at every step? The only solution that he could wrap his head around was to rope his sister in—Priya was to go along with Sulochana and tell the latter's mother, that Priya's uncle had a place in Delhi. Being a close friend of Sulochana, she did not mind accompanying her to Delhi and also to the audition, and that way, satisfy everyone involved.

'Which uncle in Delhi?' Priya asked, on being apprised of the idea by Paras. 'I am not that close a friend of Sulochana. Why should I go to Delhi?'

'You know we don't have any uncle in Delhi. I want you to do this for me, not for Sulochana. And you are not going to Delhi with her, I am.'

'What?'

It took as much persuasion on Paras's and Sulochana's part to convince Priya, as it later did on Priya's and Sulochana's to convince Sulochana's mother.

Finally, she relented only when an exasperated Sulochana cried, 'What's the use of saying you will support me if you don't!'

A week later, Sulochana and Priya waved goodbye to Sulochana's mother on their way to the railway station to board the train to Delhi, but it was Paras who left on the train.

'I hope you both know what you are doing,' Priya told them, when the train was about to leave.

'We know, don't worry,' Paras said. 'And I have gone on a college industrial tour, all right? Stick to that story at home. Thanks for the help, Priya.'

When the train left Bisalpur behind on its eight-hour-long journey to Delhi, Paras felt he was embarking on his own voyage. Sulochana was with him, looking out the window, lost in her own thoughts, for once not bothering about the gusts of wind that threw her hair into disarray.

'Where are we going to stay?' she asked suddenly, turning to him. 'As you don't have any uncle in Delhi, I presume he does not have any house there, either.'

'No, but I have made arrangements, don't you worry.'

'Do we stay in a hotel, naughty boy?'

'A hotel in Delhi? Any idea how much that would cost? These keys,' Paras said, patting his pocket, 'are to a flat in Delhi.' Getting them had been a challenge on its own. The only person he knew who owned a flat in Delhi was Gajanan's father. That meant he had to beg and cajole Gajanan for the use of the flat for a couple of days, and which in turn meant tickling Gajanan's vanity by running errands such as fetching his cigarettes and tea for him—in essence, out-toadying his usual toadies. The flat was normally rented out, but fortunately for Paras, it was unoccupied for the time being, as the previous tenant had just vacated it.

'A flat just for the two of us?' Sulochana asked, incredulous. 'What you are dreaming of is not going to happen, let me tell you right now, Paras.'

'The only thing I have in mind is rehearsing what you will say in your interview. What were you thinking of?'

'How is it my fault?' Paras was astounded. 'How am I supposed to know everything? They don't show the GDs on TV. Interviews yes, but no GD.'

'But they cannot interview thousands in two days, like that girl said. You should have thought of that.'

'Yes, it makes sense now, but I didn't think of it before, sorry. That's why we needed time to go over precisely these kind of things.'

'But you don't understand, do you?' Sulochana said, pulling his shirt fiercely, much to the amusement of another couple. 'To have come so far and then lose out like this.'

'Nothing is lost,' Paras said, sharply. 'Let's go out and have something to eat. We still have more than three hours.'

'But—'

'Shut up.'

'How dare you to talk to me like that? You think you know everything?'

After that, she did shut up and Paras had to spend the next fifteen minutes begging for forgiveness. 'I am sorry, Sulo, but I don't like to hear you being so pessimistic. You have a very good chance of qualifying. You have nothing to fear.' He knew, though, why she was petrified by the prospect of the group discussion—she would have to converse, and not merely converse, but also dominate the discussion, in English.

His conjecture was correct. No sooner than they sat at a table in the nearest restaurant they found, she became frantic again. 'What can I talk there, in front of everyone? The moment I start talking, with my English, they'll start laughing.'

'But you can't just keep quiet and watch the others!'

'At least they won't laugh then.'

'How about you talking just the way you do with me, in Hindi?'

Before she could start voicing her objections, or ripping his collar, Paras hastened to clarify. 'That's the only way, Sulo. In Hindi, you will be comfortable and you can be aggressive and dominate the discussion.'

'And how will it look when all speak in English and I go on in Hindi like a villager?'

'It will set you apart. That's what you want,' Paras said, growing excited and convinced about his own idea, the more he dwelt on it. 'You make it look as if you are speaking in Hindi because this show is in Hindi. Of course, everyone talks a mixture of Hindi–English, but you believe in the purity of language.'

'I do?'

'Sulo, you have to stand apart. You already do because of your looks. Just add some aggression and you have got it. You have to register in the eyes of the observer.'

'But what will I speak on?' Sulochana asked, apparently not too convinced by his enthusiasm. 'I should know the subject and you know how my general knowledge is.'

'Oh, come on. This is not a GD for IIM candidates. It will be some dumb topic like "What do you think about premarital sex?" and not about your views on the European economy.'

'Maybe you should give the GD in my place since you claim to know so much about it. And a little while back you didn't even know there would be a GD!'

'What are you fighting with me for? Look, there are no geniuses out here. The really intelligent people would be writing entrance exams or giving job interviews now. We are all in the same boat.' When he thought of the guy who had been attempting to break into *The Real Deal* for three straight years, and yet bragged at the camera that he was here to beat everyone hollow, he had to laugh. And when he laughed, he stopped feeling scared.

What was Delhi but Bisalpur multiplied a thousand times over? The same people, the same shops, cars and roads and buildings; bigger, wider and taller, but essentially the same. So he had no reason to feel cowed by them. Either he was as good as any of them, or they were as bad as him. No matter how you saw it, it was a comparison of equals.

That was the attitude he wanted to project onto Sulochana, so that she would lose the air of diffidence she was wrapped in, which was an antithesis to her usual personality. They munched their way through their veg biryani, overcome by pangs of hunger they had forgotten in their excitement. Paras's mind was racing.

'Let someone else begin the discussion, but you should be the second or at most the third person speaking. It is easier to react and oppose someone's opinion. Does not matter how illogical you sound, just oppose. Say you disagree because...in one or two lines. Try to be a little insulting, if you can.'

'But why?'

'Then when the first person opposes you, you jump on him. How can he attack you personally when you simply disagreed with his opinion?'

'Why would he attack me personally?'

'He would not, but you say he did. Pick a fight and put the blame on him. Choose a guy, not another girl, or the sympathy can get divided. Get me?'

'Yes, pick a fight with a guy,' Sulochana said. 'But again, why?'

'Attention, attention and attention. The observer should think—if I have this girl on my show, will she create a hungama, a ruckus, on the show? Will people want to watch her? Do anything, but just don't sit quiet there. That's the worst thing you can do.'

Sulochana did not offer any comment.

'Just keep reacting. Do not sit quiet like this there.'

'But if they are arguing amongst themselves, what can I say?'

'Doesn't matter. Just jump in.'

Chuckling cynically, Sulochana said, 'You think all of them will just be waiting for me to speak? Why would they give me a chance without taking it themselves?'

'Then complain to the observer that you are not being given a chance to be heard. That will also get you attention.' He had the answer to every question she threw at him. 'Good. Now think over the different ways in your mind how you can oppose, or—what?' Paras stopped abruptly, distracted by her smirk.

'You are just bullshitting, aren't you?'

'What?'

'The observer is there for just that, observing. He isn't a schoolteacher to whom kids complain.'

'Okay, I meant the moderator, not the observer.'

'Paras, you have never participated in a GD yourself. You don't have a clue.'

'But what's wrong in what I said?'

'Look, I know you are trying to help me, but...you know what?' She looked at him with a glint in her eye, 'I cannot plan for it this way. I will decide what to do in the GD room when I am *in* the GD room... But I am not scared anymore.'

'Well, that's great,' Paras said, puzzled by the sudden transformation. 'Just be your natural self, and you will be through.'

'You think we will have time for a movie tonight—in a real multiplex?'

'Sure, the night show should be possible.' Was she really back in her dauntless avatar, or was this change of subject an attempt to take her mind off matters that threatened to overwhelm her with fear? He decided not to probe her further.

On returning to the audition grounds an hour later, they found the scene considerably less chaotic. Many, perhaps, had finally come to terms with the fact that only the shortlisted candidates could go further now, and there was no point hanging around, hoping that the event would suddenly be thrown open to all. A continual hubbub prevailed over the ground as though on the eve of an examination.

A volunteer directed them to Lecture Room-II. A bunch of people were already waiting or prancing up and down the corridor leading to the lecture room. Apparently, the 2 p.m. GD was still going on, having begun late. A chart taped to the wall near the door listed the names of the candidates scheduled for the different GDs. Each GD had twenty participants. Sulochana ran her finger down the 3 p.m. list and located her name at number 14.

'There I am,' she said.

'So you are on this GD too! I am in it at number 15.' The guy was about a head taller than Paras, had a clean-shaven face and his eyes had a brownish tinge that made Paras distrust him instantly.

'I am Sufi,' he said, holding his hand forward to her while ignoring Paras completely.

Sulochana, looking confusedly at him and at Paras, shook his hand and said, 'I am Sulochana.'

'I wonder what kind of topic they will give,' Sufi said. 'Is this your first attempt here?'

His fluent English left Paras in awe, but he was also infuriated at the guy's act of not seeing him. Of course the bugger was trying to impress Sulochana, who appeared tongue-tied and similarly awestruck by his English and his looks. 'Yes, this is my first attempt,' she said, carefully, to avoid any mistake in her English. Did she have to shake his hand?

'Well, looks like we are competitors. Anyway, where are you from?' he asked. 'I am guessing you are not from Delhi.'

'She's with me.' Paras stepped in, and realized that he had spoken louder than he had intended. Others turned to look at them.

Sufi flinched, and this time acknowledged Paras's presence. 'Sure, I—'

The doors of the lecture room were flung open. 'The 3 p.m. GD batch, please move into the classroom,' a volunteer announced.

'All the best,' Sufi said to Sulochana and stepped into the room.

'Bastard,' Paras muttered. 'Thinks he is too smart. You don't worry about guys like him, Sulo. Total show-offs. Remember what I said. Be confident and relaxed and bindaas as you naturally are. You look the best in this group, and only two other girls are in it. So you have half the battle won already. Just be who you are, and you will qualify easily. Love you.'

Sulochana squeezed his shoulder, smiled weakly at him, and went in with a quick, timid wave.

CHAPTER 8

For Paras, the days that followed took on a strange, fuzzy nature. Like a pendulum, he swayed from vicarious happiness at Sulochana's successful qualification to the inevitable realization of his own failure. He had failed not once, but twice, while Sulo—under his tutelage, and who looked up to him and acted upon his advice at every stage, grudgingly or otherwise—had made it through the online screening, the GD and also the dreaded interview with Pepe, the de facto face of *The Real Deal* on TV.

Sooner or later, the interview would be telecast on TV, and then nothing could prevent Sulochana from turning into a minor celebrity. The last time Bisalpur had made it to the newspapers was when adulterated kerosene had caused kitchen stoves to burst in a dozen homes. The news of someone from Bisalpur making it big enough to appear on TV could not simply be swept under the carpet. But for the moment, she was contracted to secrecy with YTV that she could not reveal anything about her selection until they aired the episode with her interview.

Another secret that she had promised to keep, but without the binding of a contract, was Paras's. He wanted his attempts to get into the show to be kept under wraps as long as he was unsuccessful. Gajanan, for one, would not let him hear the end of it for years. Was he so conceited as to actually attempt to get into *The Real Deal*? He also wanted her to conceal his role in her triumph, or any connection or link to him whatsoever.

When his mental pendulum reached the extremes of its sorrowful swing, the optimistic side began pulling him back again. That joy arose from the progress he had made on the personal front with Sulochana. The two days and nights he had spent with her in Delhi were his happiest.

Finally, they had found themselves in a place where they did not have to look over their shoulders every other minute to check if someone known to them had observed them, and who would duly submit his report to his father or Sulochana's mother. No one gave a second look if they walked on the roads holding hands. And when they had had enough of the anonymity in the multitude, they had the privacy of Gajanan's flat in the evening.

The first evening they were too excited by the feat of her qualifying in the GD to think of anything else, and also daunted by the prospect of the interview the next day. He kissed her as he never had before, until he felt that her mouth was an extension of his, lips merging with lips, tongue with tongue. He tasted the food they had just eaten from her tastebuds, and inhaled a tangy peppermint vapour from her throat. Just when it seemed he could not come any closer to her, and his fingers began fumbling with the buttons of her shirt, she slapped his hand away.

'No, Paras, not yet.'

She proved surprisingly resolute and given the distraction of the impending big interview, he too hesitated to press her beyond a limit. The triumph of the second day, however, changed everything. They were to go back to Bisalpur by the night train, and returned to the flat only to pick up their luggage. But in the confines of the bedroom, Paras saw his chance and grabbed her by the waist.

Perhaps her success had made her heady, or she felt sorry for rebuffing him the previous day—whatever the reason was, Paras did not dwell on it too much because this time she yielded to him. The night train to Bisalpur was forgotten, and so was the luggage in the front room. 'You love this colour, don't you?' he asked, tearing off her top and, with some resistance, her jeans, to reveal her matching red underwear.

'Red is always sexy,' she whispered in his ear, pressing herself against him. 'Tell me you don't find it sexy.'

A loud knocking on the front door prevented him from replying. They looked at each other, stunned into silence, and held their breath, wishing the unwelcome visitor would go away. But the knocking only grew more insistent.

Paras cursed his luck as he watched the mirage of the sexy red disappear before his eyes under her jeans and top. When they were respectable again, he opened the door. A family of four including two children, saddled with half a dozen suitcases, reciprocated Paras's expression of surprise and dismay.

'Who are you?'

'Who are you?'

Paras lost his bluster when the man revealed that he was the new tenant, ready to move into the flat. The man was already at the end of his patience handling the luggage and his family, and was in no state of mind to listen to Paras. No, he would not come back in an hour. He had signed a lease with the owner and was the rightful occupant of the flat for the next eleven months. If Paras did not move out immediately, he would call up the owner and apprise him of the questionable activities afoot in his flat, the man threatened, eyeing Sulochana suspiciously. They had no option but to revert to their original plan of taking the night train back to Bisalpur, with Paras invoking the gods to rain all the curses he could think of upon the man who had interrupted their lovemaking even before it could begin.

In spite of that disappointment, just the memory of her red innerwear made Paras smile stupidly to himself in the darkness. But soon enough came the jarring doubt of how long his elation was going to last. What if he failed to qualify for *The Real Deal*? His rejection was a lot more probable than his selection. He was and would remain a nonentity, while she was well and truly on her way to becoming famous.

Once on the show, she would be closeted with the other participants, isolated from all contact with the outside world for weeks together. For her, it would be an entirely novel and exciting experience, rubbing shoulders with the smart metro guys and girls she had always admired from afar. Under those circumstances, how long would his hold over her last?

No, he was being paranoid. When he replayed that last night in Delhi in his mind, there was nothing fake about her. She loved him as much as he loved her, and who knew how far they would have gone had they not been interrupted? Sulochana knew that without him, she could not even have dreamt of such a fate. It was he who had planted the idea in her head, and nurtured it while weeding out her doubts. She had not forgotten.

But the only sure-shot way of binding her to him forever, where he would not be torn apart by his own insecurity, was if he qualified for the show too. Not only would it restore his esteem in her eyes, but also ensure that he did not became a case of 'out of sight, out of mind' for her. He simply had to qualify.

Not that he had not been trying. Delhi was a chance gone waste entirely due to his own stupidity. Had he got himself a decent haircut and not looked like the village idiot, he would at least have gained the experience of a GD. That inexperience proved costly in Chandigarh.

Though it was no secret that *The Real Deal* aspirants tried multiple times, testing their luck from different cities, the organizers made it hard for them, probably to limit the numbers. Auditions in different cities were held one weekend after another. The event at Delhi was to be followed by one in Chandigarh, and then in Jaipur. That gave Paras a window of only four to five days between two successive auditions, in which he had to apply online and reach the respective city if he was shortlisted. There was no limit on the number of times he could apply online, and even appear in a GD more than once, but if he ever made it to the final interview round and failed, he was done for that year.

While in Delhi, Paras got his hair cut, shedding the long hair ending in curly locks, the style that had seemed so cool in Bisalpur. Sulochana approved of the change. 'Now you look much better. If only you had listened to me, you could have done this earlier. Anyway, you have got rid of the Bisalpur stamp and that's huge progress.'

The new look did appear to do the trick because he got the notification mail within two days of applying for the Chandigarh round, that he was to present himself at the Khalsa College grounds that Saturday. He had not bothered to change his answers, and so it had to be his new photograph that made the difference.

Gajanan could not be of help this time around. 'Bloody hell, you expect me to have a flat in every city in India or what? My father is well-off but he is not Ambani. What exactly are you trying to do, anyway?'

'Forget it. I just asked.'

He was to go alone. There was no way Sulochana could accompany him this time, but that also meant he could put up at the cheapest place he could find without worrying about how safe or respectable a locality it was. He tried the college tour getaway trick again, but this time his father was not taken in.

'College tour again? I thought it happened once a year at most, and not every week. What are you up to, Paras? It can't be good.'

'If you have decided it cannot be good, what's the point in telling you?'

'It can't be good if you need money every week. You did not go on any college trip last week either, did you?'

Paras hesitated only for a moment. 'No.' He had nothing to lose by hiding the story of his ambition and attempts to get into *The Real Deal*. Perhaps, if he was lucky, and touched the right chord in his father, there might be something to gain instead, just like Sulochana had won the temporary support of her mother and her uncle.

Within a few seconds of his narration, however, it became clear to Paras that the said chord was sadly absent from his father's make-up. The instant he mentioned the words 'TV' and 'show', a frown creased his father's forehead. It grew wider and deeper as Paras plodded through his tale. 'So,' he concluded, 'your support will be very helpful. Just this one chance.'

His father looked at him as if he had asked for the moon. 'A TV show?' He searched for his wife but she was in the kitchen. So he repeated in the same incredulous tone, 'A TV show!'

'Yes, a TV show,' Paras said.

'Are you serious? What will people say?'

'They will be jealous if I appear on the show. For you, it will become a matter of pride. I will be covered in the newspapers and magazines and on the Internet. What more do you want?'

'You must be crazy if you expect my support for—'

'Forget it. You are right; it was crazy of me to expect your help and support and encouragement.'

'Encouragement? For this? Try studying, then see my encouragement.'

'No, thanks. I will manage.'

Somehow, he did manage to reach Chandigarh, forced to fall back on a combination of overloaded buses, trains that hardly had any standing space left and once, even a bumpy ride in a truck. All through the trip he feared he would not be able to reach in time. He made it, barely, without getting a chance to search for a cheap lodge where he could freshen up or at least dump his bag. From the bus stand he rushed to the venue in his dusty, hungry and travel-battered state, hardly in the mood to notice how the city looked more organized than Delhi.

This trip meant he was scraping the bottom of the barrel— he would be as good as broke by the time he returned home. He would either have to borrow from Sulo, who now commanded more respect at home and could get purse strings to open up, or find some other way.

The proceedings at the Khalsa College grounds were all too similar to those at Delhi, even boringly so, though scaled down in terms of numbers. The familiarity lasted until the point he stepped inside the GD room. Paras reminded himself of the advice he had proffered Sulochana, the mantra of aggression and offence that had proved so successful for her. She had scoffed at his suggestion initially, but then, finding herself ignored in the GD, employed it with devastating effect, she told him chirpily.

Once the moderator dropped the ball on the topic: 'Was it right that most of the new stars in Bollywood were the sons and daughters of older stars?', the discussion had started off in an explosion of loud voices, each trying to gain supremacy through sheer amplitude. Whether the discussion was in English or Hindi was moot, because Sulochana could hardly hear her own voice in the mêlée. When five minutes passed, and the confusion showed no sign of abating, she decided upon a gamble. She stood up, walked to the centre of the room and sat on the floor.

The moderator banged his table to quieten the noise and asked her, 'What happened? Are you okay?'

When everybody in the room was staring at her in surprise, she said, 'This seems to be the only way to make myself heard because I cannot shout as loud as the guys.'

Shamed into action, the moderator then imposed more control on the proceedings, giving everybody a chance to talk and be heard. It was Sufi, the tall, handsome guy who had cornered Sulochana just before the GD, who kicked off the new discussion, and on the expected lines that the culture of nepotism was depriving the more talented, but unconnected, from getting their due. Sulochana did not fully understand him but got the gist. So she responded, almost before he was done, that even if what he said was morally correct, it was a dog-eat-dog world they all lived in, and hence the star sons were justified in exploiting their connections and influence. If she was in their place, she said, she would have done the same, and so would he, Sufi, if he had the opportunity.

By that point, she was rid of her nerves and had begun enjoying herself. So when Sufi responded that he was certain he would not misuse his hypothetical position of influence, but he was not as certain of other people's morals, Sulochana grabbed her chance. She was scathing in the offence that she mounted on Sufi for attacking her personally without knowing an iota about her. Who was he to judge her?

Sufi went on the defensive. Others interjected in his favour or hers, but by then, she had achieved her objective of impressing the observer who sat silently in his chair in a corner in the room. Later that evening, Paras and Sulochana learnt that she was one of two people from her group to qualify for the personal interview round.

Apparently, though, it was easier to preach than to practise, or maybe he had a harder topic to debate on, or the blunt truth was that Sulo was better at it than him, because Paras soon found that things were not going the way he wanted. First, he had not hit the ground running. In spite of all his self-exhortations to stay relaxed, his nerves were jangling, and by the time he overcame them to enter the GD, the discussion was well underway. Second, there were others, brash and louder and more dominating. Third, it was not easy to counter the argument that sports other than cricket ought to be encouraged in India. He could not attack anyone because no one really responded to him. They heard him out, nodded, and carried on the original argument. Towards the end, when the discussion turned into a wrangling and shouting match, a free-for-all, where no one could be heard, the observer stepped in to break the pandemonium.

Six hours of waiting ended in an anticlimax when the list of candidates who had made it to the interview was announced, and it included no one from his GD group.

The disappointment tasted as sour as a lemon. But he could not afford to dwell on his failure. The Jaipur round was next week, and that seemed to be his last chance. Mumbai, Kolkata and Bengaluru were too far away for him in terms of both time and money, and being big cities, the competition was bound to be that much tougher.

So again, as soon as he returned home, reversing that exhausting journey but with the same discomfort, he started afresh, for the third time in as many weeks, the process of uploading his application on to *The Real Deal* website. His lack of enthusiasm was obvious even to him, and as he began keying in his answers that he knew by rote now, the monotony of the whole affair defeated him.

On an impulse, he deleted his answers and began typing in whatever came to his mind first. He wrote:

I am not going to say that I want to be in *The Real Deal* just because I believe I have it in me. It is needless to say that if you want something bad enough, you will get it, and by God, I will be in *The Real Deal*, whether it takes me three tries or thirty, one year or ten. But what is the point in saying that some day I will be on the show, even if I go broke attempting it (just as I am broke now)? Or that my father will kick me out of the house for not listening to him, but I will slave and save and try again?

No, I don't want to bore Pepe sir and the other selectors with all this stuff, which, although true, is perhaps equally true for countless others trying to be on *The Real Deal*. I am well aware of my limitations: I would be the last person to claim that I excel in academics, or that I am a natural athlete, or possess a notable talent for singing or acting or dancing or any fine art. And yet, I am capable of big things. There are some things in life that you know, that you simply believe in. My being on the show will prove it, bring me fame, and also give me a chance of living the life that I have always dreamt of.

After completing the application, Paras went to Pizza Parlour, the sole pizza joint in Bisalpur. He told its owner that he could work there every day from 5 p.m. to 10 p.m. Having a young educated college-going person to serve in his joint, on the lines of Pizza Hut and McDonald's, would enhance its status. He could commit himself to at least three months of work, but could he get a week's payment in advance?

The owner laughed him off. Paras then begged, pleaded and cajoled. He told him about his hard times, about his father's refusal to support him. Finally, the owner relented but on the condition that Paras would get his payment only after working for a week. A little more negotiation ensued until Paras convinced him to part with the money on Friday if he stayed every day until 11 p.m., the closing time.

For once, he was glad Sulochana wasn't with him. She would surely have come had he called her, but now, after the double failure at Delhi and Chandigarh, he hesitated to. It was not right to put her in a situation where she would be forced to subdue her own happiness for his sake. If she truly wished to be with him, she would miss him and call him, instead of waiting for his call. He had to leave it to her to decide. She did not call.

Initially, Paras felt odd wearing the red T-shirt and cap in the pizza place, as though he was back in school in a fancy-dress competition. But the embarrassment wore off after a while. It did not require much to welcome guests to their table, offer them a menu, take their orders, convey it to the kitchen and present them a bill when they were done; more so, when the joint was not exactly teeming with customers.

He would go there right after the last lecture in college was over. No one—Sulochana, or his gang in college, or anyone at home—was aware of what he was up to. He was too exhausted by the time he returned home around 11.30 p.m. to be concerned about his mother's worried queries, or his father's sarcastic comments.

On the third night of his midnight homecoming, he found his father bubbling over with fury. 'What are you trying to do to me?' he yelled as soon as Paras entered the house and shut the door.

'I am not doing anything to you.' Paras would rather not have answered, but he had to say something.

'You are! I met Mr Fernandes today.'

'So?'

'He said he had gone to Pizza Parlour yesterday, and that... you were working as a waiter there. Is that right? Is that what you do the whole day?'

'Not the whole day. Only in the evening,' Paras said evenly.

The more he showed his equanimity, the more his father's rage seemed to escalate. 'But why? Is that why I gave you an education, sent you to college? So that you can serve food to other people?'

'I don't see anything wrong in it. I need the money. Or would you prefer I stole or robbed it?'

'You didn't stop to think for a moment about me? People will think we are so hard up for money that I make you work as a waiter to earn! Why do you need this extra money anyway? Isn't the pocket money I give enough?'

'I told you already. I want to take part in the TV show. I need some money for that. But you said you would not give me any.'

For a few seconds, the only sounds in the room were the whirring of the ceiling fan and his father's heavy breathing. 'How much do you need?'

'Not much, Papa. Just enough to go to Jaipur for a couple of days and come back.'

'How much?'

'One—two thousand. Only two thousand.'

The journey to Jaipur, compared to the Chandigarh one, was luxurious. Having the security of enough cash in his pocket to cover any foreseeable exigency also helped Paras's peace of mind. The satisfaction was double because he had extracted his due from his father, though he told himself to be careful not to overplay his hand by making extravagant demands.

Jaipur did not have the imposing big-city feel of the kind Delhi had, but Paras was astonished by the number of foreigners at the railway station and also in the city, walking or being driven around in cycle-rickshaws. More surprising was the fact that *The Real Deal* was holding an audition here, a first in the history of the show.

Paras expected the number of hopefuls turning up to be much fewer than Delhi or Chandigarh. And when he reached the audition venue, it appeared as if his wish was turning into reality. He had braced himself for the GD, determined to get in the first or the second word as soon as the discussion kicked off. Then came the welcome news that there was to be no GD. The organizers had decided, based on the numbers who had registered and turned up, that they could screen the candidates based on the answers they had submitted online. The process would take a few hours, but after that they could get into the interviews straightaway. If they were quick enough, maybe they could even wrap the programme up in one day instead of the expected two.

Paras was sure he stood a better chance in a personal interview than in a GD where he would have to compete against nineteen others at the same time, and getting attention was a matter of chance and luck. But first, he had to be shortlisted.

A nervy couple of hours later, he found he had been shortlisted, and that his interview would happen some time late in the evening. Numb with disbelief, he turned around to look for someone he could share his joy with, but realized he did not know anyone there. At that moment, he knew he had been stupid to cut himself off from Sulochana. He missed her so badly, he wondered how had survived the last few days. He called her and gave her the news.

She squealed with delight.

'Are you happy, Sulo?' Paras asked.

'Of course. I want us to be together on the show too.'

'Really? I thought you didn't want to be with me.'

'Me? You are the one who wants to do everything alone and secretly. You don't involve me now.'

'Well, I thought you would be busy. You will become famous soon. I felt you would not want to be seen with me.'

'You are so bloody crazy. I was waiting for you to call but you didn't. How could you not, especially after what happened in Delhi?' she said, her voice dropping to an indignant whisper.

'So you still love me, Sulo?'

'I wish I could slap you for asking that. You just qualify in the interview and come straight back to me. That's what we have dreamt of, right? Concentrate on that. You remember how I did in my interview? Do the same.'

'Yes, I remember. Thanks, Sulo. I love you.'

'I love you too, my Paras Nath.'

How could he forget her wide-eyed description of the false bravado with which she had entered the interview room, and how she had almost 'fallen dead' on coming face-to-face with Pepe, the man who had made *The Real Deal* a household name. With his cold, unflinching eyes and sarcastic barbs that stung like whiplashes, Pepe had earned himself the reputation of being the rudest man on television. But she, Sulochana, sparred with him on equal terms, shrugging off innuendo-laden questions such as whether she was ready to do anything to get in and survive on the show, with a mocking emphasis on the word 'anything'.

'Anything within acceptable limits, yes.'

'And who decides the acceptable limit? You?'

'Of course I do.'

'What if I don't consider your "acceptable" as enough?'

'Look, I am sure it will be okay. You can't be suggesting anything indecent on a show that will be telecast on TV. You are just bluffing.'

That made Pepe and his co-interviewer exchange smiles, and she was vaguely aware of the cameraman behind breaking into a chuckle too. The tension in the air broke, and she knew, at that instant, that she would make it through. When they asked her what she did for fun, and she replied that she rode a 150cc Yamaha, her selection became a foregone conclusion.

Paras was well aware that he could not adopt the same tactics and get away. Sulochana was a pretty girl and that was two-thirds the battle won. She had shown her sassiness in the interview and the ability to stand out in the GD. Pepe definitely treated the girls with kid gloves when compared to how he dealt with the guys.

His interview was scheduled for later in the evening, but he dared not go away in case they changed the schedule for some reason. He hung around in the hallway that led to the interview room, observing the nervousness or bravado the others exhibited. Along with her TV crew, VJ Shivani accosted each interviewee right at the door, just before he or she went in, and as soon as they came out. The nervy ones had morose expressions and shrugs, while the show-offs flashed victory signs and broad grins.

He could not tear himself away from the place. He was hungry, but was in too high-strung a state to eat. Hours later, after going through the throes of tension, anxiety, relaxation and then indifference, it was his turn to be called for the interview. Paras felt the knots in his stomach tighten as he heard his name.

Shivani stopped him at the door. 'How do you feel, Paras… Paras Nath?'

'Oh, call me Paras,' he said brightly, realizing that this could be telecast on TV later. 'Both nervous and excited, honestly.'

'All the best, then,' she said, patting his shoulder, and screamed something into the camera.

Paras took the most momentous steps of his life to find Pepe and his co-interviewer, Sahil, an ex-'Real Dealer' himself, watching every movement of his. Pepe waved him to the sole chair facing them. He was aware of at least three cameras in the shadows, one to his front and two behind him. But he had to ignore their presence and act as if he were having a private conversation with Pepe.

Sahil began, 'Paras Nath Sharma, are you as old-fashioned as your name? Do you think you have a chance to be on this show?'

Paras shrugged. 'I hope it's not my name that decides it,' he said, conscious of Pepe's eyes boring into him.

'So you are ashamed of your name?'

'Well, I do wish my father had chosen some other name. If I had a more modern name, you wouldn't be making fun of it.'

Pepe banged the table. 'Listen, fucker, I can make fun of anything I like, your name or your face or your father.'

'Other things, yes. But not my father, sir.'

'But you said just now that you hate your father.'

'I did not. He did what he thought best, which may not have been the best for me, but that doesn't mean you can say anything about him.'

'You can't tell me, fucker, on my show,' Pepe screamed, 'what I can or cannot say! Get me?'

'I get you, sir. If our places were changed, I would do the same to you.'

'Do what?' Pepe asked.

'Call you a fucker if I had the chance.'

Sahil chuckled, and then toned his mirth down on noticing the frown on Pepe's face. 'Bloody idiot, don't get oversmart with us. I will have you kicked out.'

'Yes sir,' Paras said, wondering if he had gone too far, but then sensing that he was doing something right, because they had not acted on their threat of throwing him out. All he had to keep in mind was that Pepe was a regular guy who had happened to make it big. He appeared on TV shows, in advertisements, and even in a cameo in a movie, but underneath he was still a regular guy.

Sahil intervened quickly to salvage the interview. 'What is the most adventurous thing you have done in your life, Paras?'

'No, there's nothing...' Paras began, before realizing that they did not want to hear him calling his own life boring. They wanted to hear something interesting, and yet not so bizarre so as to sound incredible. 'I once kicked a cop's bike down right before their eyes,' he said.

'And why exactly did you do that?' Sahil asked.

'I hope they broke your nose for that,' Pepe remarked with a wry grin.

'They would have, had I let them catch me,' Paras said, and proceeded to relate the embellished story of his brush with the policemen of Bisalpur. In his narration, however, he swapped his own role with Gajanan's, such that he anointed himself as the audacious leader of their bike gang, who let a poor sap straggling behind take the rap for him.

'I don't believe you are capable of that,' Pepe announced. 'However, I will give you marks for imagination.'

Paras shrugged, as if it were no skin off his nose whether Pepe believed him or not.

'So you want to be a part of *The Real Deal* because,' Pepe said, poring over Paras's answer sheet, 'you want it badly. What English is this? Do you know the spellings of simple words?'

'English is not my strong point. You don't get exposure in Bisalpur, like you do in metro cities.'

'Excuses. If you try, you can.'

'Yes, sir, that's what I said. If you want something badly enough, you find a way. Maybe I don't want to learn good English that badly.'

'And why do you want *The Real Deal* so badly?'

'Because I have to prove that I am a capable person, that I can achieve something. I am not good at studies nor do I have a talent like singing or dancing, but still I am capable of achieving. I have to prove that.'

'So only good-for-nothings come here,' said Pepe, turning to Sahil then looking back to Paras. 'Prove to whom? Your friends or family? It's all just an ego trip then for you?'

'No, sir, I have to prove it to myself. I don't care what others think. What matters is what I think of myself.'

'That's why it is an ego trip.'

'You can call it what you like. I said, it doesn't matter what others think.'

'I think it matters what I think, duffer.'

Paras shrugged as if that could not be helped. 'It's your show.'

'Don't you think everyone else here badly wants to be in the show?' Pepe barked. 'What's so special about you?'

'They couldn't want it as badly as me.'

'How can you know about the others?' Sahil asked.

'All right,' Pepe spoke up suddenly, heaving a deep sigh. 'I am done. Let's get rid of this monkey now.'

'Monkey?' Sahil laughed. 'You are right, he does look like a monkey, a langoor. Can you be a monkey for us, Paras?'

'Sure, sir,' Paras said, staring back at them. Suddenly, he sprang from his chair, leapt onto the table, screeched and threw the papers on the table on the astounded faces of Pepe and Sahil.

'Get the hell out of here!' Pepe screamed. 'Never show me your face again.'

CHAPTER 9

The hardest part for Sulochana was the waiting. From the time of her selection in the Delhi auditions to the point when YTV would inform her that she was to proceed to Mumbai where the show would kick off, all she was supposed to do was wait. She could not even broadcast her joy, bound as she was to secrecy by a contract. The only place she could talk about it was at home, but there was a limit to which her mother was prepared to share her happiness, given that she had never been in favour of Sulochana's participation in the show. She would rather undergo the GD and the personal interview all over again, instead of this waiting and twiddling-your-thumbs period.

Only Paras could truly appreciate the sense of exhilaration in riding a big bike, under the eyes of a dozen cameras. But it had become harder and harder for her to express her joy in front of him, for fear of hurting his feelings. True, he had never reproached her, but it was easy to see the pain of failure in his eyes.

'It isn't fair, Paras,' she said, 'that I have qualified and you haven't. You have planned so much for it. You deserve it more than I do.'

'Nonsense! Anyway, I will get my chance sooner or later.'

Things had gotten to the point where she found she was always thinking about what she was going to say in front of Paras before she said it. Paras on his part, also became stiff and formal. She avoided mentioning *The Real Deal* at all in his presence, and he carried on the pretence that it did not matter at all. The frequency of their meetings and conversations tapered off. She felt helpless in the face of his reluctance to involve her in his plans.

Until, of course, the day he returned from Jaipur. He came straight to her house instead of his own. When she spied him outside her gate, dusty and sweaty and with a battered travel-bag, but with a wide grin on his face, she knew at once that the tide had turned. He nodded, too excited to speak.

Later in the evening, in the sanctuary of Bisalpur Palace, Paras filled her in. The moment VJ Shivani announced his name as the only selection from the Jaipur auditions, and the others were left shell-shocked that someone with a name like Paras Nath could actually make it to *The Real Deal*, something inside him changed.

The sense of disbelief, of incredulity, he told her, was overwhelming. His being selected for the show as one of the fourteen finalists sounded too good to be true; a dream that he would be jolted out of when he woke up.

For the benefit of the cameras, and to satisfy his own urge for theatricality, Paras had raised his arms heavenwards like a sportstar winning a tennis Grand Slam. From the high he reached then, he had hardly descended a rung. The other changes were not internal. His success established his stature at home. 'My father,' he said excitedly, 'has not raised his voice once against me. He also said, "Well done!" and might even have smiled.'

Sulochana squeezed his fingers and said softly, 'Welcome back. I missed you.'

'What?'

And then she landed a soft slap on his cheek. 'That's for going away in the first place.'

'I did not—'

'Shut up.'

'But we got what we dreamt of,' Paras protested. 'Both of us together on the show.'

'We will be on TV, my God. You in the same place as Rudy, imagine that!'

'And you in Komal's.'

Usually they sat facing each other across the table, but today Paras slid in beside her. He looked into her eyes and she could make out he was immeasurably happy.

He reached forward slightly, and before she could realize what he was up to, she felt his hand snake across her upper thighs. Getting a glimpse of the action under the table, the waiter's eyebrows shot up in surprise.

'What are you doing?' Sulochana whispered urgently. 'The waiter is looking.'

'Let him,' Paras said. 'Who's afraid?'

What was wrong with him? 'This is not a movie hall, Paras, where no one can see us.'

Paras stared back at her confidently, adamant on letting his hand lie where it was, ensconced in her lap. 'Sulo, it's okay now. You said.'

'What did I say?'

'That I can—that we can be closer once we are both out of Bisalpur. And now, thanks to *The Real Deal*, we are both out.'

Now that an understanding of his behaviour had dawned on her, she felt like giggling, amused by his impatience. 'We are in Bisalpur Palace,' she said, gently dislodging his hand from its place, 'which, as far as I know, is in Bisalpur.'

'You know what I mean!' he said, looking miffed. 'We've both escaped Bisalpur, and that was your condition.'

'Yes, I know, but let's wait till we actually get out. What's the hurry? We have our whole lives ahead of us.'

That did not seem to mollify him.

'We will have all the time and opportunity to be together on the show,' she said, trying again.

He brightened. 'Openly? I don't want to hide this from the world all the time.'

'In front of everyone. I will sit behind you on a red CBZ, and we'll zoom off waving to the camera. We'll be like Komal and Rudy.'

After indulging in similar banter and shared fantasies for some more time, Paras's forehead suddenly furrowed. 'But I don't think so, Sulo.'

'Don't think what?'

'That you and I should ride a bike together on the show.'

'Why not? That's what the guys and the girls do. Or,' she said, frowning in mock anger, 'you suddenly don't want to go with me now? Plan to find someone else there?'

'You know I can't think of any girl other than you.'

'Then?'

'We are not supposed to know each other. We just happen to be from nearby towns.'

'Are you afraid of what your parents will think when they see you on TV? You are bold when no one can see us, in movie halls or in bedrooms or restaurants, but on TV...'

That nettled him. 'It's in the contract. We are not supposed to know or have any understanding with other contestants before the show. If they find out, they can kick us out!'

'Rather far-fetched. How will they know?'

'But we can't take any risk. What if it strikes some jealous idiot like Gajanan? All it takes is one anonymous call to YTV to screw us.'

'Fine! I won't recognize you on the show. Happy? And what about the college people here who already know about us?'

'You are right. We have to stop meeting here.'

'Oh, great. Only thing is, they already know.'

Paras pursed his lips in thought. 'How about simply denying it? If someone asks, we don't know what he is talking about. It's not as if there is photographic or video evidence against us.'

So out of nowhere, mid-conversation, Paras made an about-turn. From being frustrated about her not allowing him to flaunt their closeness to the world, he turned paranoid at the thought of their being seen together. His swing from one extreme to the other exasperated Sulochana.

'Who's going to notice us, seriously?' she asked. She had to admit it was mainly Paras's resolve that let them stick to their plan. She was never fully convinced about the idea of not seeing each other, and thought that he was making a mountain out of a molehill.

They reassured each other that they had to put up with the forced separation only until the shooting began. Once on the show, they could be seen together as long as they made it appear as though they had forged a relationship only after meeting each other there.

Until then, they decided they would meet secretly in Bisalpur only in the late evenings, outside the glare of the day, and that too by arriving and departing from their rendezvous separately. In college, they did not even meet each other's eyes if their paths happened to cross.

As expected, their colleagues in college did accost them with questions. 'What happened? You people broke up or what?'

'What are you talking about? I was never seeing anyone.' Both stuck so stoutly to their denial that the others stopped questioning after a point, especially when they did not observe them doing anything to the contrary.

Eventually, after a month of this subterfuge, Sulochana was glad to receive a call from YTV that the auditions all over India were completed, and the fourteen finalists selected. They were to reach Mumbai by 20 October for the shooting of *The Real Deal*, Season 5. As before, the matter of their selection was to remain strictly confidential until the audition episodes were telecast.

Though Paras wished he could accompany her on the journey to Mumbai, both knew they could not afford being seen together before the show started. Moreover, her mother and uncle insisted that the latter escort her to Mumbai. They agreed there was no point in not humouring them at this point. What mattered now was what they did on the show, and they better devote their energies in that direction.

She did not meet Paras again until that hot, humid morning in October—though they kept in constant touch, texting and talking on the phone—when she reached Radisson Hotel in Mumbai, where she was to finally begin her journey on *The Real Deal*. It was the biggest hotel she had ever stepped into and it made Bisalpur Palace look like a slum. She reminded herself that she was in a different league now; she had to stop being overawed by grandeur.

Discreetly placed signs of *The Real Deal* directed her to the lawns at the back. At the spot pointed to by the last arrow stood Sufi, the guy who had tried to strike up a conversation with her in the Delhi GD. It was then that she remembered he was the only person apart from her who had qualified from Delhi.

'Hey! Sulochana, right?' Obviously, he had not forgotten her either.

'Right. Sufi...'

'Absolutely. So here we are at last.'

From the corner of her eye, Sulochana could see that Paras, too, had arrived on the scene. He was glaring in their direction and she guessed he was not too pleased to find her chatting with Sufi. But if he was honest with himself, she was actually heeding his advice in not recognizing him before the others and striking her own friendships. She wanted to run up to him and hug him—it had been so many days since they had last seen or met each other—but restrained herself, as though he were nothing but a stranger to her.

But they were just two out of probably a hundred other people out on the lawn. On one side, *The Real Deal* crew was getting ready, setting up their big bazooka-like cameras. A curved dolly track was laid out in the centre. There were others wielding microphones, and one man with a boom mike stretching several feet. The sound technicians were at work, barking instructions at the ones with microphones, from behind tables heaped with equipment and cables. At the other end of the lawn, a prop background of *The Real Deal* was put up, where one man was busy tidying up the area. Pepe stood out in the crowd, striding from group to group, getting their updates.

Paras could not keep himself away. He approached them slowly, and Sufi noticed him only when he was a few feet away. The critical question was whether Sufi would recognize or remember Paras from their brief encounter in Delhi, though Paras's appearance had altered a great deal since then. But this was a risk that had to be taken sometime or the other.

'By any chance, are you both on *The Real Deal* too?' Paras began. 'You are not behind a camera or a mike, so I'm assuming you're participants?'

'Yes, I am Sufi, from the Delhi auditions,' Sufi said, looking hard at him. 'And you...have I met you before?'

Sulochana found herself holding her breath. Paras blinked hard. 'I don't think so. I am from the Jaipur auditions. Paras, though people call me Percy.'

'Jaipur? All right,' Sufi said, reaching forward to shake Paras's hand, 'then I could not have met you.'

She could almost hear him heave a silent sigh of relief. His new hairstyle had come in more than handy. 'And you too?' Paras asked, turning to her.

'Yes, Percy. I am Sulochana. From Delhi too.' She avoided looking at him for fear of bursting out laughing.

'Pleased to meet you, Sulochana,' Paras said, extending his hand to her.

'Have you met anyone—' Sufi's question was interrupted by his phone ringing. 'Excuse me,' he said, moving away.

When he was out of earshot, Sulochana said, giggling, 'Really glad to meet you, Percy.'

'Phew! If he can't place me, then we are probably safe. But couldn't you find anyone other than this show-off? Or did he latch on to you as soon as he saw you? Anyway, let's each go our way and talk with the others. Enough of Sufi.'

'Hey! You tell me to act natural and mingle and now—'

'Well, mingle with others too.'

'As you say, Mr Percy! You don't have to be jealous. You are my one and only, Paras Nath.'

Pleased with her reassurance, Paras walked away from her. Telling her to mix freely with the others and watching her do it were two different things in his mind, Sulochana observed—you could take a guy out of Bisalpur but you could not take Bisalpur out of the guy. And as if he was not going to talk with other girls on the show!

The hustle-bustle around was reaching a crescendo. Last-minute checks on the cameras, video monitors and mixers were carried out, and received a thumbs-up in response from the technicians.

She could now discern more people in the lawns who did not appear to be part of *The Real Deal* crew. Sufi and two other guys were talking to a tall, leggy girl in a knee-length skirt. She walked over and introduced herself to the group. The other guys were Rohit and Victor from Mumbai and Kolkata, respectively. The girl, who was about two inches taller than her, was Aisha, again from Mumbai. Sulochana felt Aisha's gaze upon her clothes, as though sizing her up and dismissing her in a matter of seconds.

'Attention, Real Dealers!' A voice they instantly recognized as Pepe's suddenly boomed out of a mike. 'All fourteen of you are here now. We will begin shooting in five minutes. Please assemble over there, in front of that backdrop when you are ready.'

This was it, then. The thought seemed to strike all of them at the same instant, as they all mirrored each other's expression of excitement mingled with fear. Rohit gave words to their feeling when he whispered hoarsely, 'This is it, guys. All the best.' Their quest, from which there was no turning back now, began here.

Pepe received the final go-ahead from a man who Sulochana guessed would be one of the production managers of the show. The cameras were ready to roll. 'Action!' The cry rang aloud, followed by an unnerving silence.

Pepe stepped forward, peering at the array of *The Real Deal* finalists before him, taking his time in playing to the camera. 'Guys and girls, welcome to *The Real Deal*, Season 5, the most popular reality show on Indian TV for the last four years, on the most popular youth channel, YTV. Thousands of youngsters all over India try to be here. Only fourteen of you have succeeded. You are happy to be here, aren't you?'

A shy chorus of 'yes, yes', was heard.

'What? I didn't hear you. The Real Dealers cannot shout?'

'Yes sir!' Much louder this time in a collective scream.

'That's better,' Pepe said. 'I want to see the *Real Deal* spirit. You know the *Real Deal* spirit, right?'

'Yes, sir.'

'Good. Never give up, always put up a fight, even if you know you will lose. That, in essence, is the *Real Deal* spirit.'

Sulochana found herself near the centre of the row, with a guy and a girl, both of whom she had not met, on either side. She was curious to see who her other competitors were, but did not want to miss a single word of what Pepe was saying.

'I am sure all of you know the rules of the game. Survival. The last man or the last girl standing is the winner. People get eliminated through vote-outs. After every vote-out, there is one person less competing on the show. At the end, when thirteen have been eliminated, we will have one winner. Clear?'

Solemn nods followed, the yells of 'yes, sir' forgotten.

'So, at the end of thirteen episodes, one of you will be crowned the winner of *The Real Deal*, which is a guarantee for nationwide fame and attention of the people who matter—TV, movies, ads, what not. I am an example before your eyes. Do you agree?'

Again, they nodded. It was not an empty boast. Pepe might not be as big as a Bollywood star or a cricketer, but you would be hard-pressed to come up with a more popular face on TV. The movies too, would follow, sooner rather than later, given his pre-existing fame. Perhaps not the ones that wanted the chocolate boy hero, but the ones with the rugged-looking action heroes would be more in his line.

'But more than the fame and the spotlight, what you will relish most is the feeling of winning, of being the best among the best. Being known as the winner of *The Real Deal* is an unbeatable feeling. Again, take my word for it. However, if that is not enough for you, there's the money. Maybe not crores like *KBC*, but a good deal of money for your age. With our growing popularity and sponsorship, we now have an increased total prize money of Rs 16 lakh.'

Gasps, hoots and whistles ensued. There were around a hundred people in the background, with the cameras and the mikes, those who had put up the sets, painted them, the ones directing them, and those trying to coordinate and make sense of it all.

'If you go out in the first vote-out, you get Rs 100.'

Giggles. Snickers.

'Yes, a laughing matter,' Pepe said. 'If you don't accept your prize money, it will go to a charity. With every round, the prize money gets doubled. So, the second person voted out gets 200 bucks, the third gets 400 and so on. By the time you reach the final stages, the last three places are worth Rs 2, 4 and 8 lakh. That is, the winner gets 8 lakh. Is that a laughing matter now?'

'No, sir,' someone feebly replied.

'So that's the incentive for you to stay on as long as you can. The more episodes you last, the more you win. You can work out the maths, I hope. Of course, you won't have any concept of an episode. For you, there will only be tasks and vote-outs. You don't get to see any TV or have any contact with the outside world, once we begin. We will take away your mobile phones or any other means of communication. We will also take away your money and cards so that you will have no means outside of what we give you. No books or magazines or games or any other entertainment is allowed, so that twenty-four hours a day, you will be a part of *The Real Deal*. Your stuff will be returned to you when your stay on the show is over. You will sign a contract with YTV that lists all these terms and conditions. Anyone found violating the terms will be thrown out of the show immediately, with no prize money. Any questions so far?'

Silence.

'Good. Everything will be transparent here. The rules are rules and will not be changed. You will get what I promise you. People who go out won't turn up like a bad penny through wild-card entries or some such trick. No gimmicks to raise the show's TRP. You won't have all kinds of tasks like money tasks or advantage tasks or immunity tasks. All tasks here are just survival tasks. If you win a task, or are part of a team that wins a task, you cannot be sent out in the next vote-out. But if you lose a task, or if you have done well individually but your team still loses the task, bad luck. You are vulnerable and can be voted out.

'The tasks will be fair. It will pit equals against equals. No unfair advantage of physical strength or gender can be used. Who votes you out? Every remaining participant in the show has a vote. The one who gets the most votes against him or her goes out. Fair?'

'Yes, sir.'

'What happens in case of a tie?' someone asked.

'Good question. Then there will be a tie-breaker task to decide that. How you vote a person out depends entirely on you. It might have nothing to do with your performance. If others don't like your face and gang up against you, you are out. You do your best in your assigned tasks to be safe, but if not, then you have to play the game, plot or scheme, whatever it takes. But you cannot offer any incentive outside the game. That is, you cannot tempt another person by offering him money or anything else outside the show. Any such thing will lead to instant disqualification. Clear?

'All your scheming and thinking or discussing has to happen on camera. You cannot make strategies off-camera. People found doing this will be thrown out, and with no money, even if it is in the final round. I am serious. Be fair about the game, and I will be fair to you. Clear again? Cameras will be in your face and following you all the time, except from late night to early morning, when you are supposed to sleep. And no, the cameras will not follow you into the bathroom.'

Giggles.

Pepe rubbed his hands together as though warming them before a fireplace. This was his trademark style, and now Sulochana was watching it live.

'All right, Real Dealers. The tasks will be difficult and can be dangerous, but our crew will attempt them first to make sure they are doable and safe, if the necessary precautions are taken.

'You will not interact with the crew in any way. Your only contact, other than your fellow contestants, will be me. Clear?

'You must have seen previous seasons of *The Real Deal*. This is not a place for the faint-hearted. You will drive long distances on the road on your bikes. You will wear helmets all the time and will not do any rash driving. If anyone is scared and wants to leave, now is the time to say so. You are free to go home. We have replacements ready. Anyone scared? Anybody wants to back out?'

'No, sir!' They would all rather die than back out now.

'Great. Now get ready to form your teams. Guys, pick up your lots from here, and girls, from there,' Pepe said, indicating two bowls on a table, a few feet from him. 'These will tell you which team you belong to.'

One by one, they walked up to the table, picked a slip from the appropriate bowl and announced their name and team number.

Mohinder:	Team 1
Sheetal:	Team 2
Rohit:	Team 1
Rashmi:	Team 1
Rithik:	Team 2
Naureen:	Team 2
Irfan:	Team 2
Prabhjot:	Team 1
Percy:	Team 1
Aisha:	Team 1
Sufi:	Team 2
Sulochana:	Team 2
Victor:	Team 1
Chetan:	Team 2

Just before Sulochana returned to her place, after announcing her team, she winked at Paras. Sufi, standing beside Paras, caught the wink, assumed it was for himself and winked back. Paras, about a head shorter than Sufi, stared ahead deadpan as if he hadn't noticed anything.

'That's it for now,' Pepe announced. 'Elect the captain of your teams and give your teams a catchy name. You will get your first task when you reach your first destination. And for reaching there, you have your awesome Hero Honda Hunk bikes...right behind you!'

They turned around, and found, as magically as a rabbit jumping out of a hat, an array of gleaming red and black bikes.

'Wow!'

'Happy? You have eight bikes, four for each team. Six of you ride in pairs, while one has to ride alone. Clear so far?'

'Yes, sir!'

'Wonderful. *The Real Deal* journey, Season 5, begins now. Your journey on the road starts from here, Mumbai, and by the time we reach our final destination, Delhi, we will have our winner. Have fun, but ride safely. Tomorrow, things turn serious.'

CHAPTER 10

'The Black Mambas' was the team name Rohit came up with. Paras was not too taken by the fact that their team was named after a deadly venomous snake (something that Rohit had to explain to him), the reference to the movie *Kill Bill* being lost on him. 'Whatever. It's only a name,' he said, when his opinion was sought, shrugging it off as one of those 'metro' fancies he could not wrap his head around. It was as good, or as bad, as the name the other team, of which Sulochana was a part, had chosen—'The Crouching Tigers', yet another allusion to a foreign movie.

The thing that mattered was the team composition, and Paras decided he had no reason to be unhappy with his. Their skipper Rohit was obviously their biggest asset, given his physique, looks and smartness—the complete package, one could say, along the lines of Rudy.

Mohinder was another big, strapping lad. If a task boiled down to a test of sheer physical strength, the combination of Rohit and Mohinder would be hard to beat. The third guy in their team, Victor, was definitely not in the same league, but then, probably the others held a similar opinion about Percy.

His first impression of Victor was that he was a bumbler—he had already dropped the bike once, even before starting it. Of course, he could be wrong about him, but it appeared as if the girls in his team—Aisha, Rashmi and Prabhjot—shared his opinion, as all three were reluctant to sit behind Victor on the bike.

That pleased Paras, as he did not want to cut a lonely figure right at the beginning, riding by himself. Unfortunately, that left Prabhjot to ride with him, as both Aisha's and Rashmi's eagerness to be with Rohit was painfully obvious. Aisha prevailed, and so Rashmi went with Mohinder, trying hard but failing to conceal her disappointment.

Prabhjot, who along with Mohinder was the selection from Chandigarh, snorted in disgust. She had the build of a shot-putter or a discus-thrower, with a voice to match, and was well aware that she could not compete with Aisha or Rashmi as far as looks were concerned. 'Shameless. We haven't even started, and they are already fighting over guys.'

Paras chuckled. 'Let them.'

'Hey, Prabhjot, want to come with me?' Victor asked, butting in.

'Only if you don't drop me,' Prabhjot said. 'Thanks.'

Paras could only look on open-mouthed as Prabhjot joined Victor on his bike. Victor's small stature contrasted with her physique made them a funny sight, but Paras did not feel like laughing. He was the one riding alone now.

'Ready, guys?' Pepe yelled. 'A part of our crew will be in that Innova, going ahead of you, who will film you from there. You all need to follow it. If it stops, you stop. Clear? Now, go!'

Surely, they did not film these instructions Pepe gave them. Percy guessed that the cameras would be on all the time and capture everything, and only later in the editing room, they would decide what to cut out. Pepe flagging them off on their bikes with a chequered flag was bound to be shown. But what was the point of bothering about these things that were anyway out of his control and, more importantly, did not matter?

Perhaps riding alone was a blessing in disguise. He did not have to bother keeping up small talk with the others, as he could see Prabhjot jabbering away in Victor's ear. Instead, he could observe others from a distance, and try to identify their respective strengths and weaknesses. Or, he could simply forget about the game, and pause for a moment to appreciate where he was.

He had succeeded in getting in where thousands of others, as eager, smarter and more intelligent than him, had failed. He was out of the clutches of obscurity and Bisalpur, doing something that he loved to do—riding a jazzy bike—in a show that would be telecast on national TV. Paras, or Percy, rather, would become a household name.

Sulochana sat behind Sufi—something that he had half-expected and half-feared, yet seared his heart, nevertheless. He would not have minded as much had she been sharing the bike with any other guy. She probably did not have much choice in the matter, unable to refuse her captain, while itching to ride the bike herself.

The problem with Sulo was that she was so easily awed by the slick airs of the metro guys. At the auditions, all Sufi had had to do was spout a line or two in English for her to stand gawking. Had she been in his team, they could have cooked up some excuse to ride together. Instead, it was Sufi who had usurped his place, literally, on the rider's seat of the bike, while he was the one who had dreamt, months ago, of zooming off into the sunset on a bike with Sulo. It wasn't fair. But he had to steel himself to the sight, which was perhaps only a precursor of what would follow. Was that little quirk of fate—Sulochana picking up the slip marked Team 2 instead of the one marked Team 1—going to have such a momentous impact?

Having this big bike under him was a dream, and assuaged his hurt to an extent, though they were forced to go at the sedate pace set by the Innova ahead. It was like riding an elephant: the gentle, swaying ride belying the monstrous strength of the beast.

Barely ten minutes and two kilometres into their ride, the Innova rolled to a halt, and the crew shooting them from the back waved at them to do likewise. They pulled over to the side and waited until a minibus caught up with them. Pepe disembarked from the bus and said, 'Had fun driving? Now, leave your bikes and get into the bus. Your bikes will follow you to your destination—Nashik—in a pick-up truck.'

This announcement was met by incredulous reactions from *The Real Dealers*. 'You are kidding, right?' Sufi asked Pepe.

'We haven't even hit the fourth gear!' Rohit said.

Pepe grinned. 'Sorry, folks, but we cannot risk you fellows meeting an accident on a four-hour-long ride on the highway. So you hop on to a safe and comfortable ride on our minibus.'

'But we want to ride our bikes,' Mohinder said.

'And all the previous years the Real Dealers rode their bikes,' Chetan said. 'Why this change for us?'

'Believe me,' Pepe said, still chuckling, 'this is how it has always been. The audience is not interested in watching you ride a bike for hours. You feel good, but it's not good for the viewer. What they are interested in is seeing how you perform the tasks, how you play the game and the vote-outs. And,' Pepe continued, 'we have enough footage now to show that you rode your bikes all the way. You will ride the last mile or two before we reach our destination of the day, and we will shoot that too. So, on TV, you will both leave and arrive on your bikes. Clear? Now, into the bus, please. We are already late.'

'The bikes?' someone asked.

'Leave them where they are. The crew will take care of them. They have to be with you when you ride into Nashik.'

On the show, Pepe's word was law. All of them filed into the bus, sighing and shaking their heads. Paras was disappointed as his bike was wrenched off his hands just as he had started getting a feel of it, but he also could not help admiring the trick played by *The Real Deal* producers. Obviously, they had been successful in making him believe all these years that Rudy and Komal spent hours whizzing past beautiful scenery on their bikes. He could never have guessed in a hundred years what actually happened behind the scenes.

Once in the bus, however, Paras found that travelling together gave him a much better opportunity to get to know the others, even those from the other team. Almost all of them were college-going. Only Rohit and Rithik were graduates, and the former the only one with some actual work experience. Again, barring Rohit, none of them was over twenty-three; almost everyone else fell in the age bracket of nineteen to twenty-one.

'All right, let's play antakshari to pass the time,' Rohit said, when they were settled in the bus. 'Guys against girls. No point just staring out of the window for the next few hours.'

Paras felt like snickering at the idea. As though they were schoolkids out on an excursion! But he noticed that no one else was laughing. They followed the suggestion without a murmur, the girls and the guys segregating into groups, as if it were Pepe commanding them. No wonder when Pepe had asked them to select the captain of their team, the choice of 'The Black Mambas' had been unanimous. Rohit was clearly the one who garnered attention and faith in his ability, without even having to try. Some people, Paras thought, were born to lead.

Only Mohinder matched Rohit physique-wise, but where Rohit was suave and stylish, Mohinder's Jat rusticness stuck to him like a second skin. Paras was glad that Mohinder was on his team, and he would not have to compete against him in any physical contest.

Among the girls, Aisha was easily the most beautiful, both teams considered. She was miffed when she began to sing 'My heart must go on', but was told that only Hindi songs were allowed. 'I am sorry, I don't watch stupid Bollywood films,' she said, and from that point on, kept her nose pressed against the window, taking in the scenery outside. Her haughtiness showed that she was well aware of her looks and the advantages that went with possessing them.

The English the others used did not turn out to be as critical a factor as Paras had feared. Most of the time they conversed in Hindi. If they did start off in English, and Paras was not certain what they meant, he waited long enough until he was sure he got the gist, and then joined in, steering the conversation naturally into Hindi. His high point was when he remembered a song in the nick of time to save his team from losing a round.

A milestone revealed they were close to Nashik. About a kilometre from the place they were to be put up in, they had to play out the same charade they began with, in reverse. As dusk fell, the bikes were unloaded from the pick-up truck, and forming the same pairs they had started out with, they drove behind the Innova up to their guest house.

The guest house was an independent bungalow on the outskirts of the city and thus ideal for shooting. The guys got the two larger rooms, four from each team in one; the girls went three into each, again according to the team composition. But there was no rule forbidding them to mingle among themselves.

Pepe had announced a welcome party later in the evening, a night filled with song, dance and booze (the guys assumed), where all the contestants could get to know each other better. The guys had hardly settled, throwing themselves onto the beds to stretch their feet out after the long journey, when two crew members walked in with a camera and a mike.

'Sorry, guys. No talking outside the camera.'

Victor groaned. 'How are you going to show twenty-four hours of footage on TV?' Mohinder asked.

'Leave that to our editing team. And please do not talk to us. Forget we are here. You just talk among yourselves, about the game or whatever you want, as Pepe has said. You will get used to us.'

Indeed, it was as they said—if you ignored them, you did forget their presence, as though they were a part of the furniture, a ceiling fan or a wall clock. They went about their jobs professionally, neither intruding nor reacting in the slightest way.

Soon, it was time to get ready for the party. Paras tried not to be conscious of the difference in his best shirt and the branded clothes the others unpacked from their suitcases. In the evening, he hoped it would be too dark to make out the contrast. The girls, when they turned up at the party, were decked in all their finery. Aisha, in particular, preened like a princess, as if expecting the others to fall at her feet. Paras found his gaze drawn time and again to the shapely legs she displayed below her short skirt.

He tried his best to open up and mingle with the others, to erase their prejudice that he was a loner, but somehow felt unable to get through, as if they had put up a protective shield against him. On observing that the only cameras present were looking at the party scene from afar and not following anyone in particular closely, he sidled up to Sulochana during a rare moment when she was alone.

'You are looking beautiful,' he whispered into her ear.

Startled at first, but then realizing that this was a private, stolen conversation, she smiled. 'Thanks, Paras.'

'I miss you, Sulo.'

'So do I.'

'Really? I thought you were too busy with Sufi to miss me.'

She drew in her breath sharply. 'Paras! Not again. It's only talking.'

'Just talking?'

'Of course. How does it compare with our Bisalpur and Delhi and everything between us? Have some trust in me.'

'But we were to ride together, Sulo.'

'I know, but we are not in the same team. We can't explain riding together. What can I do, Paras, tell me?'

'But at least, do you—'

'Hey Sulo! One dance?' Sufi had emerged beside them out of nowhere.

'Oh, Sufi, I don't know the ABC of dancing.'

'It's nothing. You will learn in five minutes. Just follow my lead.'

The words of her reassurance to Paras paled before the sight of her learning dance steps from Sufi. And Sufi, much as Paras hated to admit, was the best dancer in the group.

The rumour about the free booze was true, and Paras helped himself to a bottle and a half of beer. They returned quite late in the night. The recording crew left soon after, reiterating the rule about not discussing anything related to the show off-camera.

Almost as soon as Paras's head touched the pillow, he thought he heard a loud banging at their door. Rohit, who was already up, opened the door to reveal a surprisingly bright sky outside, and a new pair from the TV crew. Pepe was the one threatening to blow the door down. 'Your first task. Get your team ready. We meet outside in exactly ninety minutes, and ride to the venue.'

That got everyone up and running helter-skelter to the bathroom to get ready. Paras locked himself in the bathroom after waiting patiently for his turn that came last. Standing under the shower, he felt a little better after having woken up with a heavy head. He knew he should have restrained himself with the beer. But at least he had been better than Victor, who had made a fool of himself after gulping three glasses and asking Naureen for a dance, when she was clearly not interested.

He heard more voices from the room; perhaps the guys from 'The Crouching Tigers' had joined them. Their first task would be upon them soon! Feeling excited at the prospect, Paras whistled a merry Bollywood ditty but the tune froze on his lips when he heard the name 'Percy' spoken outside.

He realized that no one was yelling at him to come out, but they were talking about him, thinking that he could not hear them over the pattering of the shower.

'—don't like Percy,' someone said. 'He's too quiet.'

'I think he's an okay guy.' Paras recognized Mohinder's deep voice. 'He's not from a metro so probably feels shy.'

'Did you see how he was guzzling away the beer just because it was free? Cheapo!'

'It's not that. I just don't trust guys who keep silent,' the first unidentified voice said. 'Everyone can play that game, remaining in the background and just observing others, without revealing anything of themselves.'

'True, if Pepe has selected him, it means he is not dumb.'

'Right. Saw how happy he was riding the bike alone? Then in the bus ride he sat by himself, and then again in the party last night, standing in the corner, and watching the others. I say let's observe him for some time, and then...'

The conclusion was inaudible, perhaps sealed over a solemn shaking of heads. Paras, dumbstruck, stood frozen under the shower. Keeping a low profile did not mean nobody noticed him.

He emerged a few minutes later, rubbing himself with a towel. Only 'The Black Mamba' guys were in the room; the owner of the unidentified voice was absent. 'I am done. Who's next?' He ought to be able to put faces or names to voices. He had to know who was against him right from the start, and on whose support he could count.

The venue for the task was barely a ten-minute ride away from the guest house, and they did not have to go through the rigmarole of loading and unloading the bikes. The crew, a big group of about sixty to eighty people, was already at the site, and appeared to be ready. Other bystanders, drawn by the presence of the cameras and with nothing better to do, joined the scene. Apart from a camera on an elevated platform that would provide a bird's-eye view of the proceedings, no fancy props like huge cranes or pulley contraptions were to be seen.

The only visible indication of their task was a set of four parallel chalk lines on the ground. The two inner lines were in yellow, about fifty feet apart, while the outer ones were in white, with a hundred feet between them.

They could only guess at their purpose while Pepe went around talking to the crew and getting their go-ahead. Sulochana stood apart with her team, looking animated and fresh, showing no sign that she had had only four hours of sleep. The smile she threw in Paras's direction wiped out all the serpents of jealousy writhing in his heart since the previous night's party. At that instant he was ready to fall in love with her all over again.

'Good morning, Real Dealers!' Pepe's voice boomed out, as he stepped forward and took on his favourite stance of rubbing his hands in glee. 'So, all of you had a grand time last night? I am sure Victor enjoyed it.'

Everybody laughed while Victor looked sheepish.

'Today,' Pepe continued, 'we start off the business end of *The Real Deal*, Season 5. Something you have been eagerly waiting for, to prove yourselves. Haven't you? Now is the time to actually justify the big words you threw at me in your interviews and application forms. Ready?'

'Yes, sir!'

'The task is quite simple. You see these two chalk lines in white? All that each team has to do is carry over as many flags as it can, from one line to the other. The team that carries the most flags in ten minutes is the winner. Which means, none of the winning team members can be sent out in the first vote-out. Simple?'

'That's it?' Sufi asked. 'Just carry flags from here to there?'

'That's it,' Pepe said, an evil grin threatening to break out on his face. 'Oh right, I forgot. One person can carry only one flag at a time. Three people from both teams will stand at either end, beyond the white lines. The seventh person coordinates and manages from one end, like a goalkeeper shouting out instructions to his players in a football game. The people at one end try to hand over the flags to their team members at the other end. This handing over must be done within the centre yellow lines, which we will call the exchange zone. After receiving a flag, the person goes back to his white line, plants the flag there and comes back to the exchange zone for the next one. Clear?'

'Yes, sir.'

'You have to give the flag only to your teammate, and not to the other team.'

'But why would we give our flag to the other team?' Rohit asked.

'Didn't I tell you? That can happen because, except for the coordinator, all of you will be blindfolded.'

'Oh, God!'

Pepe waited for the cries of surprise and despair to subside. 'That's right. There will be plenty of confusion because there will be twelve of you in the exchange zone to give or receive flags. You cannot call out names or make any sound.'

'Then how will we identify who's a teammate?'

'That's for you to decide your signal. No looking, no talking. Captains Rohit and Sufi, you have two minutes to decide who will be the coordinator from your team, and which three on which side, or any other strategy. Your time starts now.'

The teams quickly formed huddles, soccer-team-style. Rohit asked, 'Any volunteers for the coordinator role? There will be a lot of running around to get and plant the flags. The coordinator will mainly have to stand at one end and direct the others. So whoever can't run fast can be the coordinator. Aisha? Rashmi? Any of you?'

'Yes,' Aisha said. 'I can do it.'

'So can I,' Rashmi said.

Paras took a deep breath. It was time for a gamble: either he stepped forward and contributed, proving he was a team player, or tried to remain in the background, hoping to get overlooked. 'We will be blindfolded,' he said. 'No one can run around. The coordinator's role will be the most important one.

All of us should be able to hear and make out his or her voice. One of us guys, or Prabhjot, can you do it?'

'Yeah, I think I can shout louder than all of you!'

'Are you sure?' Rohit asked, looking doubtfully at Paras and Prabhjot and then at Aisha, who was beginning to look sore.

'I think Percy has a good point,' Mohinder said. 'We have to walk fast, not run.'

Mohinder's assent tipped the scales. 'All right, Prabhjot, you be the coordinator,' Rohit said. 'You give us the flags and shout at us to go left or right or forward or back. Mohinder, Percy and Rashmi be on this side to take the flags; while Aisha, Victor and I will be on that side to receive the flags, clear? And we shake hands with two hands, like this, with the other person, to identify a "Black Mamba". Do not hand over the flag if you do not feel two hands around your hand. Okay?'

'Clear.'

'I still think I can do a better job than her,' Aisha said, pouting.

'You chose me as your captain. You have to go with my decision,' Rohit said, looking hard at her. 'All the best, guys. Let's go for the win.' To Paras, more softly, 'I hope your idea works.'

Rashmi could not hide her delight at the rebuke Aisha received from Rohit.

On dispersing from their huddle, they found that 'The Crouching Tigers' were already taking their positions. They had gone with the idea of making who they felt was their weakest link—Sheetal—as their coordinator, because apparently they did not consider it an important enough role.

Soon, all but Prabhjot and Sheetal were blindfolded. The black ribbons covering their eyes were broad and thick. Paras could not see a sliver of light through or under it. The last glimpse he had was of Sufi, Sulochana and Chetan being led to the white line on the other side, along with Victor, Aisha and Rohit.

When Pepe's whistle pierced the air, Paras grabbed a flag from Prabhjot, and strode rapidly towards the yellow line, which he estimated would take him about twenty big steps. This was the moment to stay calm and not let overwhelming yet useless thoughts, such as—oh God, this was it, his first actual task on *The Real Deal*—crowd his mind.

Plenty of cameras were covering them from every direction, some in wide angle, and some in close-up shots, with the cameraman hovering nearby. He would see what the cameras saw weeks or even months later, when it would be finally aired on TV. For now, the only thing that mattered was Prabhjot's voice screaming out directions. 'Percy, forward a few steps and then to the right. Mohinder, to your left. Victor, come forward. Percy is just on your right. Reach out. Come on, give him the flag, Percy.' Paras reached out, touched Victor and shook his hand to make sure, before giving him the flag.

'Well done, Percy, now hurry back. Back, back! Mohinder come back to your right. Rohit, no, that is their team. Come back! Aisha, left, left.'

Prabhjot's voice easily dominated Sheetal's. Only when Prabhjot was not yelling, could Paras make out Sheetal faintly, like a whisper in the wind. He rushed back to Prabhjot to collect his next flag. It got easier if he followed her instructions though occasionally she goofed up and he bumped into others.

In all, he collected six flags and successfully handed them over. Once, he shook hands with a girl, but she did not return his two-handed shake. He was not sure if it was Sulochana. But the moment passed quickly with Prabhjot screaming at him to move on.

Pepe's second whistle marking the end of ten minutes blew when Paras had just collected his seventh flag. He was confident they had done well because of the number of times he had heard Prabhjot cheering as compared to Sheetal; but then Sheetal was not always audible. When their blindfolds were taken off and they tallied their counts, they found they had collected sixteen flags, though Prabhjot was sure she had seen eighteen.

Pepe called everyone to order and attention. 'How did everyone find the game? Great? So let's count the flags now, and know who wins, and which means, who is safe tonight.'

'"Black Mambas"—in your allotted time, you collected and handed over sixteen flags, but two of them were disqualified. One was outside the exchange zone and one was given to your opponents. So your net count is fourteen. Okay? Do you think that is good enough to win?'

'Yes, sir,' Rohit said. 'I think we did well.'

'Let's see. "Crouching Tigers". You collected and handed over fourteen flags.'

Silence.

'So if all of them were correct, there's a tie.'

'Yes, sir,' Sufi said.

'What do you think? Were all of the exchanges done correctly?'

Paras wished Pepe would stop playing around and announce the result, whatever it was. When they would telecast the task on TV, this was most likely the point at which they would take a commercial break, only in order to heighten the viewer's suspense. The tactic certainly used to keep him on the edge of his seat when he would watch the show on TV.

'However,' Pepe rambled on to his conclusion, 'you handed over one flag outside the exchange zone, and so that will not be counted. You have thirteen flags in all. "The Black Mambas" win.'

'The Black Mambas' duly erupted in joy, with high-fives and hugs galore.

'Congratulations to "The Black Mambas". The first vote-out will be tonight. None from "The Black Mambas" can be voted out, but anyone from "The Crouching Tigers" can. Be ready, folks.'

The first vote-out was a novel experience in the sense that it was their first, but there was nothing unexpected that unfolded in it. Word had come around from 'The Crouching Tigers' through the girls that Rithik was the marked one. 'The Black Mambas' had no reason to oppose the decision, and so the nomination was accepted without any objection. Somehow, Rithik had consistently rubbed everyone the wrong way because of his bragging.

The mood among 'The Black Mambas' was upbeat as they had nothing to be apprehensive about. Plenty of jokes were cracked at Rithik's expense, many of them to do with the fact that he was the namesake of a superstar. But secretly, Paras was sure, each of them was dreading the day he or she would be in Rithik's place, when everyone around you knew that you were the marked one, except yourself.

Perhaps that realization made them a little sombre in the night when they collected at Pepe's bidding. The backdrop was similar to the one in front of which they had started out in Mumbai. They stood along with their bikes, waiting for Pepe to begin the proceedings.

Pepe asked them to come up one by one and cast their votes, that is, write the name of the person they wanted out of the show. After milking the suspense as usual, he finally got down to counting the votes. And then: 'So who among "The Crouching Tigers" suspects he or she will get voted out today?'

Irfan and Sheetal raised their hands.

'Why do you think you will be voted out?'

'I think others are jealous of me,' Irfan said.

This statement was received with plenty of chuckles and sniggering from both the teams. 'As if you have anything to be jealous of,' someone muttered.

'And you, Sheetal?'

'We lost because of me today. That's why.'

Probably tiring of dragging on the game, Pepe abruptly started reading out from the stack of votes in his hand. 'Rithik,' he said, startling Rithik and nobody else.

'Did you expect this, Rithik?'

'No, but one vote is fine. I am not worried.'

Pepe nodded. 'Rithik.' 'Rithik.' 'Rithik.'

After the fourth blow, Rithik got a grip on reality. He turned philosophical. 'It happens. The world is like that. People you trust betray you. I think I know who is behind this.'

'Who?' Pepe asked.

'Doesn't matter. Let the others find her out later when they get betrayed like me.'

'So you suspect it's one of the girls? But there are so many votes against you?'

Rithik shrugged, while the others giggled, having shed any trace of guilt they might have felt earlier.

The final scorecard read: Rithik 13, Sheetal 1. The only vote that did not go against Rithik was obviously his own.

'Why, what did Rithik do to all of you in such a short time?' Pepe asked, pretending to be amazed. The rest either stared at the ground or smiled back enigmatically. The only thing that mattered at that moment was that it was not them going out. Some shook hands and waved goodbye to Rithik, and some even gave him a parting hug when the car that would escort him out of the venue drove up.

'So that was your first vote-out,' Pepe said. 'One down, twelve more to go. Tomorrow, we ride.'

CHAPTER 11

A period of one week, when compared to the average human lifespan, is insignificant. But Sulochana found it hard to believe how much difference one week could bring about in her life. The transformational moment, of course, was the instant her entry into *The Real Deal* was confirmed, but until the day the shooting for the show began, nothing inside her had changed. To others, she showed off a devil-may-care attitude, but her heart still quailed at the thought of confronting the world she had only glimpsed on TV so far.

Only after surviving for one week on the show did she start believing that she was in her rightful place. This was the change from within, and it mattered because she knew it was real. One whole week of *The Real Deal* meant she had been through three survival tasks and three vote-outs. Rather, three tasks and one vote-out, because she was effectively immune in two, as 'The Crouching Tigers' had won two tasks in succession after losing the first one.

Her survival also meant that she had played her part in the team. She did not fail her teammates; she was not squeamish about crawling through muck and messing up her beautiful hair, unlike the other girls. She did not flinch outwardly at the sensation of creepy-crawly insects on her skin, though she was close to gagging. Sufi had praised her on camera to Pepe, and the praise made her glow.

After losing the first task, 'The Crouching Tigers' were apprehensive of the disadvantage of being one member short, and thus losing out on subsequent tasks, a position from which it would become increasingly difficult to recover. But that was not how the events played out. They now had the upper hand in terms of numbers.

Paras, too, had somehow survived—those eliminated from 'The Black Mambas' were Victor and Rashmi. After every vote-out, where either Paras or Sulochana was at risk, when they found they had both emerged unscathed, they exchanged glances filled with relief and joy. Neither had envisaged being on the show without the other. And so, to find their dreams intact even after three vote-outs filled Sulochana with happiness.

Once Rithik was ousted from her own team, it left the remaining guys and girls well-paired. They could make do with three bikes, but seizing her chance, Sulochana said she would be glad to ride a bike on her own. She had no problem taking anyone—guy or girl—pillion behind her, but ride she would.

Even when she showed her licence to Pepe, he remained sceptical about her riding a heavy bike on the highway. 'This isn't a Scooty, Sulochana. It's a Hunk. A Hunk, for God's sake!'

But Sulochana was adamant. 'I told you on the interview itself that I ride a 150cc. It's not as if we ride hundreds of kilometres. Just a few in the beginning and at the end, right?'

'Remember,' Pepe said, 'it's your responsibility.'

'Yes sir, I know I have signed the contract. If I kill or injure myself, it's all my fault.'

None of the other girls dared sit behind her, and neither was any guy willing to give up the chance of riding his own bike, or perhaps they felt they would look silly sitting behind a girl on a bike called Hunk. Either way, Sulochana was not displeased, because she had the bike—a red one, of course—all to herself. She had driven Paras's Splendor before, so she was used to its gear sequence, which was different from the Yamaha she rode back home. Riding the Hunk shoulder-to-shoulder with Sufi, catching his appreciative glances, or the envious ones of the girls, only added to her pleasure. She was the centre of attention, and she sensed that the cameras tracked her more often now. Her happiness was complete when, after giving up the bikes to go sit in the minibus, Sufi caught a moment with her and whispered, 'Cool, Sulo, really cool.' The compliment was genuine because he had not said it for the benefit of the camera.

In her bed, when the cameras and mikes were taken away at night to give the contestants a respite for a few hours, and she was finally left to her own thoughts, Sulochana wondered why it was important to her that Sufi maintain a good opinion about her. Could the only reason be that Sufi was her captain and, if she was in his good books, he would protect her from being voted out?

Sufi's opinion mattered, and not merely because he was the captain of her team, but because he easily stood head and shoulders above the other guys in 'The Crouching Tigers'. She was glad that Rithik the loudmouth was gone, and that she was the one who had initiated the move to target him. Irfan thought he was a ladykiller and could make the girls swoon simply by subjecting them to what he considered were amorous glances. Both Naureen and Sheetal readily agreed with her assessment of the guy, and Irfan quickly became a laughing matter to them. He only had to look at one of them when all the girls would suddenly burst into peals of laughter, leaving him sore and puzzled.

Chetan was a schemer, and not a good one at that, though obviously he rated much higher in his own opinion. Finding a moment alone with her, after the first task, he had whispered furtively to her that they ought to get together and vote Rithik out. To listen to her own idea coming back to her, appropriated by someone else, annoyed her. But she played along, and let Chetan belabour under the impression that he was the Machiavellian strategist.

No, she knew rather well that Sufi's captaincy could not be the only reason, or she would not be asking herself such a question in the first place. She could put on an act in front of the camera, or the others, but she had to be honest with herself.

Sufi was smart and handsome; suave and polished. His upbringing showed. His father was the managing director of a large pharmaceutical company in Gurgaon, and his mother a well-known psychiatrist in Delhi. He was never denied anything he wanted, and yet he wasn't the least bit spoiled. Only a fool would deny his attraction. There, she had said that.

Neither could she deny that he gave her special attention. When she had wanted to ride the bike, he was the one who backed her before Pepe. When she committed some gaffes in English, as she was wont to, now and then, he did not laugh at her as the others did, but quietly corrected her later, when the others were not around.

Apparently, her awareness of Sufi's attractive qualities was not limited to her mind alone. Paras was jealous of him, and about her closeness to him. She could sense, without even turning around to look, his furious gaze upon them when she was with Sufi, and being in the same team, she was bound to be thrown together with Sufi a lot more than with Paras. On his part, Sufi had not altogether got over his suspicion of having met Paras before, outside the show. Sulochana was careful to avoid mentioning Paras or her college or the place she was from because if Sufi came to know of the Bisalpur connection, it would set his antennae tingling.

At such times, Paras would rebel against his own idea of keeping their relationship a secret and forming new ones on the show, which they could exploit whenever the need arose. He asked her to curtail her interaction with Sufi, but later, on thinking over it, encouraged her once again to earn Sufi's trust.

He had been displeased with her attention-grabbing stunt of riding the bike alone, because he felt it had put her in the spotlight too early on in the game. But later, he had come around, accepting the fact that the same strategy might not work for both of them. Or that the centre-of-attention strategy was more suited to her than to him.

Later again he cautioned her, as the number of contestants grew fewer, there would be no escaping attention. At that point, they would have to think of other ways to remain in the game. But they had quite some way to go to reach that stage. In fact, he cautioned further, though they ought to think ahead, they should not get ahead of themselves either and risk falling into a ditch under their nose while gazing at the horizon. Sulochana, growing weary of his cautions and warnings, wondered if he relaxed even for a moment to enjoy simply being on the show.

She could not help noticing a subtle, yet distinct, change in him. Back in Bisalpur, his life had revolved around her. Whatever he did, like burning his pocket money on her as if he were a millionaire, or holding her hand whenever he could, was motivated by the idea of getting closer to her. She spurred his dreams. Heck, he would never have thought about being on *The Real Deal* if not for her.

She sensed a kind of withdrawal in him, a lowering of his passion for her. Remarkably, she could throw back at him the very charges he made against her, either through his reproach-filled glances or in the rare instance he found her alone without a camera eye tracking them. That she was not paying him the attention he used to; that she was getting carried away by the spotlight, by the buzz of the cameras and the microphones hanging on to each act or word of hers. That she seemed to be revelling in the company of other guys. That she was not used to this liberated environment where she could do as she pleased and with no one around to question her. The very air was making her heady, and already making their shared vows of being together forever slowly fade away into the past.

Wasn't she justified in reflecting similar questions back to him? That ever since he had overheard someone talking about observing him, he had become paranoid about being voted out? His mind was unable to accommodate anything outside survival tasks and votes, so carried away was he by the show.

If he did not like her proximity to Sufi, what did he have to say about his camaraderie with Aisha?

Now, on the show, he was living his own life. He was planning and dreaming of a future on his own, and maybe even independent of her. She could observe him only from a distance, given that they were in opposing teams. It hurt her a bit to see him laugh and kid around with Aisha—the attention that was due her, diverted to someone else. She missed his devotedness, his tiresome yet flattering attempts to hold some part of her in his arms, as though, through the sense of touch, reassuring himself that she would be near him always.

But again, she did not want to dwell too much on her life back in Bisalpur, if she could help it. Certainly, there was Paras to remind her, but she was loath to reminisce about home and her mother and the parochial confines and outlook of the place and its people. Sooner or later, perhaps in a few weeks, or even days, if she was unlucky, she would have to return.

Perhaps, after the episodes were telecast, she would have the liberty to act as she pleased, having earned the right by being the first person from Bisalpur to feature on national TV. Her father, had he been around, would have made it bearable, because he would have been happy in her happiness. He would have understood and felt proud of her achievement.

That it was a new world out here became clear to her on the very first day. Her sitting behind a handsome hunk like Sufi was a matter to be flaunted, to be shown to the world later on, and not something to be clandestine about, by hiding her face in layers of her dupatta. Riding her own bike earned her the others' appreciation, and not scorn or mockery like it did in Bisalpur. The bolder her dresses grew, the more the cameras dwelled on her.

She had felt hampered by her limited wardrobe until a moment of epiphany when she recalled Komal's hot avatar on the show the previous year. Borrowing a pair of scissors from the crew, she set to work on her jeans. Sheetal could only gape as Sulochana sheared off the legs a few inches above the knee.

'What are you doing?' she asked.

'What does it look like I am doing? Getting myself new clothes!' Sulochana said, holding up the torn-off denim shorts to the mirror.

The awkwardness of exposing her legs in public left her after a few minutes. Paras's eyes grew as round as saucers, and it was fun to see the other guys' gaze stray every now and then to her legs when they thought she wasn't looking.

Even if, for a moment, she forgot about the guys and the bikes and the dresses, nothing could erase the sheer joy of travel, the open air of freedom that she breathed in the places she had been to, and the people she had met. She had stayed in a luxury hotel in Mumbai to start with; in a palatial guest house in Nashik; in a village near Dhule, off National Highway 3; and even in a cottage on the banks of the Narmada river; visited the ancient palaces and canals of Mandu, the temples near Indore and Ujjain. Could she imagine this life of adventure and thrill without worrying or being told to worry about studies and career and marriage if she was in Bisalpur?

The question was rhetorical because the answer was evident. There was no way she could take up the thread of her life at the point she had left it, on returning from *The Real Deal*. A few weeks ago, she had not dared imagine such a life—a multitude of cameras following her and a host of mikes recording her voice, for the purpose of telecasting it on national TV. Now that she was here, living a dream, she had to make it count. She could not allow it to remain a novel and pleasant experience of a few weeks that she would look back upon with nostalgia and nothing else all her life.

She adopted the video diary—the clips where one talked about one's impression of the show, about the experience, and mostly about the competitors, directly to the camera, as though chatting with the TV audience—as her confessional. As this shooting was done in seclusion, others would not come to know what she said, and so there was nothing to hold her back from airing her true opinions. Sulochana poured her heart out there, while taking care not to mention any detail of Bisalpur. Probably the only part to make it to the final cut would be of her shedding tears reminiscing about her father, about her wanting to do well on the show to live his dreams. The TV crew and the episode director hovering behind the camera soaked up the display of raw emotion like greedy sponges.

She would be foolish if she let go of the chance she had grasped. For that, she had to concentrate on the game unfolding around her, and come out of her dream-like, idyllic state. She had to keep a watch on those she considered a threat to her survival.

Sheetal was the one she was least concerned about, not finding a single redeeming characteristic in her that could have led to her selection in the show, especially as she was from a big city like Bengaluru. She must have done something out of the box in her interview, unless Pepe wanted to throw in a perfectly ordinary and boring candidate into the fray for the sake of variety. Seldom would she disagree with anyone or even participate in bitching about the others, or share her opinion about the guys.

Though Sulochana found Aisha's narcissism and sassiness intimidating at first, she felt confident about handling her if it came to that. She had observed many a contestant like her in the previous seasons of *The Real Deal*, who were too self-absorbed and worried about how they looked on the show to bother about any long-term strategy.

Naureen, though, was cut from a different cloth. She was neither bitchy nor trashy, nor considered herself a prima donna as Aisha did. She did not indulge in doublespeak, but did not shy away from airing her views if she felt she had to. Her voice was usually soft, and yet could become firm when she wanted it to be. And, Sulochana had to admit, she was beautiful in an old-fashioned classical sense. Her coal-black hair grew long and straight, she did not dress up or try too hard to look good, because her dignity and poise gave her a different kind of attractiveness. Like Sulochana, she was not daunted by the crawling-in-muck task, whereas Sheetal and Aisha were in tears. But somehow, she had managed to look graceful even through that, her bright smile, despite the mud-streaked face, winning everyone over.

Sulochana was not as confident about outsmarting or outshining her as she was about the other girls. She would need a novel approach to tackle the quiet yet forceful dignity of Naureen that seemed to affect the guys in a positive way.

To survive as long as possible on the show, her eyes had to be open, and ears sharp, to catch what Pepe was saying, as he went over the details of their next task.

'... task number four. There are eleven of you now, five with "The Black Mambas" and six with "The Crouching Tigers". Sometimes, a bigger team is better, sometimes not. You have to identify your strengths and what is needed for the task. You see that pulley contraption we have put up? This is a task of balance.'

A strong rope went through the pulley with a scale at one end, and a large can on the other. Under the can was a pit filled with water.

'You have to lower the can into the pit. The way you raise that water is not by pulling on the rope but by standing on the balance. The heavier you are, the more water you can raise. Get me?'

'Yes, sir.'

'The other members in your team have mugs with them to take out water from the can and pour it into another measuring can, placed there,' Pepe said, indicating a barrel on the ground about ten feet away from the pulley set-up.

'The objective of the task is simple. The more water you can raise and transfer from the can to the barrel within five minutes, is the winning team. Mark my words. I have not said that only one person should stand on the balance and the rest do the water transfer. How you divide your team is up to you, what you feel will work for you.

'So, are you ready, captains Rohit and Sufi? Who goes first, "The Black Mambas" or "The Crouching Tigers"?'

Both Rohit and Sufi said they wanted the other team to go first.

'Lots it is, then,' Pepe said, 'as usual. The second team probably has an advantage on whether to use the same strategy as the first team, or a different one.'

Rohit and Sufi drew slips, and Rohit turned out to be the luckier one.

' "Crouching Tigers", you go first,' Pepe said. 'Do you think you have lost the advantage by going first?'

'Maybe. But we are better off in numbers.'

'Numbers may not always be advantageous,' Pepe said. 'You should know. You were down by one after the first task, yet came back strongly in the next.'

'Let's see how it goes,' Sufi shrugged. 'We can all talk about it till the cows come home, but what matters is how you do the task. We will give it our best, like real Real Dealers. Won't we, team?'

'Yeah!' Sulochana screamed along with the others, though puzzled by the part about cows coming home.

The consensus was that Sufi and Irfan, being the heavier members in their team, ought to weigh enough together to bring up water in the can, and also hold it up long enough for the others to bail out water from it in the mugs. With four of them doing the bailing and the running to the barrel, the idea was that they would be able to transfer more water quickly, allowing Sufi and Irfan to heave up the next canful of water.

The idea was sound in theory but not in practice as they soon found out once the task began. What they had not taken into account was the narrowness of the mouth of the can. The can itself was voluminous, but its neck was narrow, like a pot's.

With their combined weight, Sufi and Irfan were able to heave up the filled can to a height of two feet above the ground. Sulochana, Chetan, Sheetal and Naureen crowded around the can with a mug in each hand, and duly discovered that only one could draw out water at a time. Two could put their hands in, but the mouth was wide enough for only one to draw out a water-filled mug. So while there were four of them hovering around screaming at each other to hurry up and give the next person a chance, the confusion was compounded by Sufi and Irfan's yelling that the others needed to hurry up the process. When their time ran out, Sulochana knew they had messed up the task.

'The Black Mambas' had learned their lesson watching 'The Crouching Tigers', as was evident by their contrasting strategy. Mohinder, Rohit and Paras got on to the balance, leaving Aisha and Prabhjot to transfer the water. Both carried two mugs each, filled one after the other, and hurried to the barrel while the other person was free to fill her mugs. With three guys on the balance, they could hold up the water can indefinitely. They also knew they had to fill just about half the barrel to be a clear winner over 'The Crouching Tigers'. At the end of five minutes, they had filled three-fourths of it.

'The Crouching Tigers' were resigned to their defeat as Pepe announced the results with a smirk on his face. 'I guess there was no number advantage today, Sufi?'

'No, we screwed up. Simple,' Sufi said. 'A collective failure.'

'You are right, you guys screwed up. So see you tonight at the vote-out, where one of you will pay the price for this collective failure.'

The last time their team had been vulnerable to a vote-out after the first task of the season, word had quickly spread that Rithik was the intended victim. This time, after losing the water can task, Sulochana waited for word to arrive from Sufi about whom they planned to gang up against. When the expected message did not come around until the evening, she brought the question up in the girls' room, to Sheetal and Naureen.

A few uncomfortable seconds later, Sheetal said, 'No, I have not heard either.'

'Me neither,' Naureen said.

'That's strange,' Sulochana said, struck at the same instant with the horrific hunch that she was the marked one. That explained her not hearing about whom they were going to vote out. Sheetal and Naureen must have heard. They knew, of course. Hadn't they exchanged a look when she asked them? The uncomfortable silence was not because they did not know what to reply to her, but they must be tearing themselves up inside dying not to laugh aloud in her face.

No, she should not panic yet. Her only hope lay in Sufi. Surely he couldn't be party to the decision. She knew her performance so far had been satisfactory. If anyone had to go because of his or her incompetence, it was Sheetal who was solely responsible for the disaster in the first task. She would confront Sufi and force the truth out of him. If they wanted her out, they should let her know instead of backstabbing her.

She went over to the guys' room and beckoned Sufi. She did not care if the crew followed them with a camera and mike.

They were just doing their job and whatever they showed on TV months later could not affect the game now.

'So am I going out, Sufi?' Sulochana could not contain herself as soon as they were out of earshot of the others. 'Just be frank. I will appreciate that instead of my finding out tonight at the vote-out.'

'Whoa! Hold on, who told you that?'

'I know it. I can read the signs because I am not dumb. But why me? If I have not performed, fine. But I have. I am the only girl here who can ride a bike. I am at least better than Sheetal or Chetan, you know that.' At this point, Sulo found her voice breaking. 'I did not expect this from you, Sufi.'

'You crazy or something?' Sufi stared at her, an incredulous look on his face. 'I didn't even think about you for the vote-out. Didn't Naureen tell you? I asked her to pass the word to you. It's Sheetal.'

'Really? She didn't tell me.' Sufi's expression convinced her he was telling the truth. Suddenly, she felt a lot lighter and sillier. 'Maybe because Sheetal was always around.'

'There you go. I know you are a performer. Why would I want you out, silly? You are the last person I want out.'

'Thanks, that is good to know,' she said, relieved. She really ought to have more confidence in herself.

But a few hours later at the vote-out, a painful jolt ran up her spine when Pepe, after his customary routine of asking who was afraid of being sent home, read out the first vote. 'This one is a surprise, I must say. Sulochana. Did you expect it?'

A horror-stricken Sulochana could only shake her head, looking at Sufi, and then at Paras, as though they were to blame.

But the next four went to Sheetal, and Sulochana could feel her heart beat slow down to the normal rate. One vote went to Chetan and one to Irfan, but the rest went against Sheetal.

Sheetal went out with an air of resignation, and a minimum of fuss, as if surprised that she had survived so far. The only thing that nettled Sulochana was that someone had voted against her. If it was Sheetal, she did not have to worry any more. Maybe it was Aisha, finding her a threat to her status of being the queen of the pack. But if it was not, it meant there was someone still on the show who wanted her out—and worse, she had no idea who it was.

CHAPTER 12

The first thirty minutes after waking up belonged to him. It was the only half-hour in the next twenty-four that Pepe could claim as his own. The rest were spent either facing the camera, getting ready for it, behind the camera, or going over the day's shoot in the editing room with the episode director. But he would not have had it any other way.

Pepe believed in being positive. What was the point of turning sour about the world, when you could not do much to change it, and spoil your own life in the bargain? But his customary cheerful start to the morning was clouded when he remembered the phone call from the previous night. Such calls would not normally be forwarded to him, but the caller had frantically insisted that he had some highly valuable secret information pertaining to the show, to reveal. As soon as Pepe answered the phone, the voice at the other end began: 'Paras and Sulochana both are from the same place. They know each other from before.'

'What? Paras who? Percy?' Pepe asked, before growling, 'And who are you? How do you know?'

'I am from Bisalpur too. Doesn't matter who I am.'

'I won't take you seriously unless I know who I am talking to.'

A pause. 'You can make enquiries if you like. I am not lying. My name is Gajanan Choradiya.' The line went dead.

If there was anything Pepe hated more than being lied to, it was not knowing he was being lied to. He took pride in getting into the skin of a contestant. They thought they could outwit him, but he was always one step ahead of them, knowing who was sincere and who was a pretender just out to impress him. And now, he had been lied to by a chit of a boy and a girl, so smoothly that he never suspected them. Assuming, of course, that the tip-off was true. Well, he would know that soon enough because he had already sent for Percy and Sulochana through a crew member, with the accompanying instruction that no one else was to know about the meeting.

The first to arrive was Paras. He looked confounded at being summoned in such a secret manner to Pepe's room.

'What's the task, sir?' he asked, looking around. 'No cameras here...'

'Why, Percy, can't you perform without a camera covering you?'

'No, sir, it's not that. I—'

'Wait a minute. You are not alone in this task.'

Pepe was not going to be taken in by that innocent, confused expression. Twice already, he had underestimated Percy—first, at the interview, and then once the show began—convinced that he had no chance to succeed. But he had been proved wrong both times, and that should have set his antennae tingling with suspicion.

Whatever doubt Pepe had about the tip-off was removed when Sulochana came in. The glance that she exchanged with Percy on seeing him, one filled with surprise, curiosity and fear, told him all he wanted to know. No amount of subsequent vehement denials on their part could erase that loaded glance from his mind.

'The reason I have called the two of you is to give you your next task. And that task is to pack your bags immediately and leave for your hometown, Bisalpur.'

Their second glance only confirmed what the first implied. After what seemed an eternity, Percy recovered to an extent to ask, 'I don't understand, sir. What happened?'

If he weren't angry, he would have found Percy's defence comical. 'You know what I am talking about but let me ask a straight question. Let's see if you have a straight answer. Do you both know each other from before the show, but chose not to reveal it to me? You help each other by making strategies together outside the camera?'

'I don't know what you are talking about, Pepe sir,' Paras said.

Pepe sighed. 'I thought you were more intelligent than this.' Turning to Sulochana, he said, 'Somehow, I am more disappointed in you.'

Sulochana lowered her eyes, unable to meet Pepe's glare. He was being truthful. Sulochana was a natural before the camera. Many people knew that the best way to act before the camera was to pretend as if it wasn't there, but few could practise that. Only once in two or three seasons did he come across a contestant like that.

Pepe was impressed with the speed at which she had adapted. Coming from a small town, he knew she could not have worn the dresses she did on the show before, as perhaps Aisha would have. But within a day she was acting as if she had been wearing cut-off shorts and short skirts for years. And of course, both the camera and the audience loved to dwell on a confident young woman who was not shy of showing off. If she stayed long enough on the show, she would develop a following of her own among the audience. She was a TRP booster, without a doubt.

'All right, since you both have nothing to say, go ahead and pack your bags. I will have a vehicle drop you at the station.'

'Pepe,' Sulochana began and stopped short, looking at Paras.

'What? Don't waste my time. I have to get on with the show with the remaining Real Dealers.'

'Please don't send us home like this,' Sulochana said, almost in tears. 'Give us one chance.'

'So you admit you were cheating.'

'Shut up, Sulo!' Paras hissed.

'Don't piss me off further!' Pepe yelled in Paras's face. 'I can find out every detail whenever I want to. Your only chance lies in your being honest for once.' He didn't know why he said that. Did he really intend giving them a chance?

Percy did not miss the implication. 'Yes sir, we knew each other in Bisalpur. But we will do anything you say. Just please don't send us back.'

'Not like this, Pepe,' Sulochana added. 'I am fine if I go in a vote-out, but not this...'

'Please sir, it's our dream to be here.'

'How close were you back in Bisalpur? Just friends, or something more...?' Pepe let his expression imply the rest.

Both nodded, Percy meeting his gaze, Sulochana dropping hers down to the floor.

He should have expected this, yet, the revelation of Sulochana's and Percy's relationship took Pepe by surprise. What could Sulochana have seen in him? Percy, to him, was already an overachiever, by virtue of getting selected for the show, and even surviving on it so far. Going by the team dynamics he had observed until now, he would have thought it more likely for Sulochana and Sufi to have a thing going between them.

He definitely got the vibes that something was developing between the two, as the episode director had observed and informed him excitedly. Nothing like an undercurrent of romance between two popular contestants to spice up viewer interest. These developments came off best when they were natural. He did not believe in resorting to underhanded methods of scripting or stage-managing these things, which he knew other shows did.

Unless, of course, it was all part of a plot, with Sulochana playacting to keep Sufi on her side. That would make her one of the most consummate actors he had ever come across. If he were in Percy's position, he probably ought to be a worried man.

Maybe, the thought struck him all at once, he could take advantage of this development. If the Sulochana–Percy link had the potential to stun him, imagine the impact it could have on the audience. Moreover, sending two contestants out together—one of them an attractive, popular girl—did no favours to anyone. Either he came out with a convincing reason that explained their sudden exit, or he revealed the true reason, which would only make him look foolish. Then he would have to conjure a gimmick like a wild-card entry to make up for the loss of contestants, and he had stated on camera that he detested such twists. Or plan for a few extra episodes that did not involve vote-outs with the remaining contenders—not an interesting proposition.

'Well, you guys cheated me by hiding your relationship and plotting outside the camera,' Pepe said. 'The only way I can let you both stay on is if you don't hide anything from the camera. Not your relationship; not your plotting.'

'And from the others?' Percy asked.

'I don't care about the others. Just hide nothing from the camera.'

'Yes, sir. Whatever you say, sir.'

'Thank you, Pepe,' Sulochana said.

'I hope you realize what a favour I am doing to you. If you mention this meeting to anyone, it will be your funeral. Now get out.'

Pepe was sure they would appreciate the favour he had done them. The relief on their faces as they scurried out of his room was palpable. They were mere kids. And yet they had fooled him.

He did not consider himself a pushover. In fact, the image he meticulously cultivated and perpetrated on TV was the very antithesis of a pushover. No one dared trifle with him. And yet, he had let the duo off with barely a slap on the wrist. Was it because Percy reminded him of his younger self, a teenaged Pepe buried in an obscure town, but with stars in his eyes? A gauche Pepe, who through a painful struggle and often embarrassing trial and error before his city-bred rivals had finally made it to where he was, thanks to a lucky break given by a senior actor in some magnanimous moment?

But one break was enough. Pepe resolved to keep a closer eye on Percy and Sulochana. Should they again try to defy his instructions, he would boot them out, regardless of the spot it would put him in.

Of the two, Percy was the one he could not quite fathom. Was he a simpleton who had stumbled onto a series of fortuitous turns, or was he one who made his own luck? When he reviewed the early episodes in the studio, including the shots that had been edited out, he found that Percy was the more cautious one, rarely, if at all, acting in a way that betrayed the fact that Sulochana and he were not mere acquaintances on the show. Sulochana, on the other hand, was not as circumspect. One might wonder why she looked frequently in Percy's direction, but only if one was on the lookout for such telltale signs.

So that evening when Pepe reviewed the day's shooting, he was pleasantly surprised to hear Percy tell Sulochana, when there was no one else around, 'Sulo, one of "The Black Mambas" will go out tonight, as we lost the survival task, and I want Rohit out.'

'Rohit? Your captain?' Sulochana was incredulous. 'You can't send him out!'

Pepe was pleased. The boy had learned his lesson. He was now following *The Real Deal* rules, and he was playing for higher stakes.

'So? There's no rule that the captain becomes immune from vote-outs. The thing is, I won't have a chance as long as he is around,' Percy said.

'But I think we got the word that we put Aisha out. That's what Sufi said.'

'Well, convince Sufi to change his mind. The others do what Sufi says, right?'

'True.'

'And Sufi does what you say. So pull your strings with him and vote out Rohit. Tell Sufi it will work in his favour. Rohit is his biggest rival. If he gets the opposing captain out, the opponents, that is us, will be shattered and lose every task. It will be a master stroke, tell him.'

Sulochana stared at him, eyes wide with surprise. 'Boy! Whose side are you on?'

The episode director paused the action on the screen and looked askance at Pepe. 'Isn't this Percy dude acting too demanding with Sulochana? I didn't know he knew her so well.'

Pepe shrugged. 'Maybe they have something going on. Let's play along and see what happens. Could be interesting.'

The director resumed playing.

'I am on my side, that's all,' Percy said. 'I will get some votes from my own side so that we are sure to get him out. Can you do it?'

'I will try.'

'No, no trying. It has to be all five votes, otherwise don't try it. Let me know at the vote-out if you have been able to manage it. Depending on that, I will go against Rohit or Aisha. I dare not oppose Rohit openly.'

'But why—'

'Just do it, Sulo, please. And don't tell anyone the idea came from me. It should not be traced back to me.'

'See?' Pepe said. 'Told you this would be interesting.' He could only guess at Percy's motive, but he thought he had a fair idea. His talk in the morning with Sulochana and Pepe must have scared the daylights out of him. Percy must have realized how close he had come to being kicked out of *The Real Deal*, and decided to gamble now that he was in his, Pepe's, crosshairs. He was ready to come out of the shadows.

In his next video diary, Percy revealed as much, though careful not to disclose anything about the confidential meeting with Pepe. 'It's time,' Percy said, looking seriously at the camera, 'that the others get to see the bad side of Percy. Enough of being a goodie-goodie boy.' Then taking on a smug expression, he added, 'I think I have a good understanding with Sulochana. I will exploit that and get what I want.'

When Sulochana carried out Percy's wish to the letter, perhaps the only ones who were not surprised were Pepe and Percy himself, though both put on a poker face, Pepe while announcing Rohit's ouster and Percy while receiving the announcement. There were exactly six votes against the dumbfounded Rohit.

So Sulochana could get Sufi to do what she wanted merely by talking to him sweetly for five minutes. Perhaps that was what Percy was wondering, thought Pepe—how much power she had over Sufi, or conversely, how much Sufi was willing to be influenced by her. The result was in front of him: Rohit, for the first time ever, lost his equilibrium. Initially, he was too shaken to react, but when the realization eventually sank in that he was going back, he raged bitterly.

'I did not expect anything better from "The Crouching Tigers", but someone in my own team has stabbed me in the back. Oh, go to hell, all of you. I don't care for this stupid show and stupid people. I have better things to do in life than lying and betraying other people you call "friends".'

Rohit shook hands with 'The Crouching Tigers' but refused to look at his team.

'It wasn't me, Rohit,' Mohinder said.

'Nor me,' Paras said, quickly. Prabhjot and Aisha reiterated their innocence.

'Fine,' Rohit said, 'I voted against myself. Bloody liars. Goodbye.'

Pepe was sad to see Rohit go. He had been the most mature contender on the show, and easily one of the favourites. But how many times had he seen the same scenario unfolding, where someone was simply too good to last?

Later, Pepe caught up with the fallout of Rohit's exit.

Mohinder had beckoned Percy, Aisha and Prabhjot. 'Do any of you have any objection if I become the captain now?'

'No,' the girls said. Percy's hesitation showed on his face, but he followed suit.

'It's not my plan to usurp Rohit's place,' Mohinder said. 'I only want to avenge his going out by sending out those who conspired against him. Because we all know he did not deserve to go.'

Pepe expected Mohinder to be shell-shocked, or show a bit

of anger, but not the intensity of rage that he exhibited now. One would think he was the one betrayed, and not Rohit.

'Mohinder,' Percy said, 'I think "The Crouching Tigers" planned it because they knew Rohit was so good. I can find out whose idea it was on their side.'

Mohinder nodded. 'Find out and tell me. Then see, the next vote-out...but someone else—'

'Let me find out first,' Percy said. Later that night in their room, Percy revealed the outcome of his investigation. 'It's Chetan. It was his great scheme.'

'The bastard!' Mohinder spat, getting to his feet. 'I will—'

'Not like this. Put him out in the next vote-out. For that we have to win the next task.'

'I promise you we will win. Don't worry about that.'

'And Mohinder, you know one of us voted against Rohit. It could be any of us four, you or me, or the girls.'

'Me? Are you mad?'

'Look Mohi, I know I did not vote against Rohit, and nor did you. So it must be one of the girls.'

'The girls?' The scepticism in Mohinder's voice was evident. 'I thought they were all crazy about Rohit.'

'I don't know. Probably Prabhjot. Maybe she did not like Aisha's closeness to Rohit. Who knows how a girl's jealousy works? Just my guess. I will try to find out.'

'Okay. First I want Chetan out, then whoever the traitor was on our side.'

In the next task, Mohinder was as good as his promise. The task clearly favoured the one with brute physical strength and thus was right up Mohinder's alley. He was so worked up that he more than compensated for the numbers advantage 'The Crouching Tigers' had. He did not care if he strained his back, or his hands bled, and to no one's surprise, 'The Black Mambas' won because no one else could match his intensity.

In the ensuing vote-out, Chetan went out and Mohinder whooped with joy as Chetan bid farewell, baffled by Mohinder's animosity. When Mohinder finished celebrating, Percy took the opportunity to hiss into his ear, 'From our side, it was Prabhjot. She's the traitor.'

Pepe decided that he liked this new avatar of Percy, more so because he felt responsible for his transformation from the lose-himself-in-the-background strategy to being a behind-the-scenes manipulator. How long he could continue playing the game without showing his hand would be interesting.

If Mohinder had badly wanted to win the previous task so as to be in a position to send Chetan out, he now contrived to lose the next task, to put Prabhjot in a vulnerable position. So obsessed was he with avenging Rohit's betrayal that he did not care if he himself would not be immune to being voted out if his team lost.

The task Pepe set them was to walk through rings of fire that grew progressively smaller in diameter. They would have to carry mugs of water in both hands without spilling. The team that did the most trips in the allotted time would be the winner.

Mohinder managed to stumble and spill most of the water in two of his trips, so that they would not count. But he need not have tried to lose as Aisha, petrified by the heat and the leaping flames, would have lost them the task anyway. Percy and Prabhjot did reasonably well but they had no chance to win, given that their own captain was intent on losing. 'The Crouching Tigers' won by a canter.

'Good. I want Prabhjot out,' Mohinder told Percy as soon as they were back in the sanctuary of the boys' room.

'But she did okay in the task. Aisha was the one who lost it for us.'

Mohinder looked levelly at Percy, fingering the stubble on his chin that seemed to sprout within hours of his shaving. 'I know that. That's not important to me. I want Prabhjot out because I don't like schemers. We owe this to Rohit.' And then he thumped the bed so hard that its frame creaked. The guy had the strength of an ox.

'What harm did Rohit do to the bitch? He was fair to her like he was to everyone. That's what I liked about him as a captain.'

'But I don't have any proof that it was Prabhjot,' Percy said. 'It's all based on hearsay.'

'Of course, here everything is based on hearsay. *The Real Deal* is not a court of law. What you say is good enough for me.'

'Fine,' Percy said, giving in with a nonchalant shrug. 'I will tell Aisha then to vote against Prabhjot, and just so that Prabhjot does not suspect anything, tell her to vote Aisha out.'

'Do as you like. But make sure Prabhjot goes out.'

As decided, Percy first talked to Prabhjot and told her that they were to vote against Aisha. Prabhjot nodded in understanding. 'She really screwed up today, big time. Fine.'

'Good. Now send Aisha out. I will tell her we decided to vote against you, just so that she does not suspect a thing.'

'All right,' Prabhjot said, chuckling. 'You guys and your scheming.'

'Not me,' Percy said. 'The captain's orders.'

When Aisha came out, Percy repeated the exercise. Aisha's relief was palpable, as she was expecting to be voted out after her disastrous role in the day's task. 'To be frank,' she said, 'I think I deserve to stay on the show longer than Prabhjot does.'

'You are right. Now let me catch someone in "The Crouching Tigers" and pass on the word.'

He caught Sulochana. Sulochana shrugged. It was all the same to her whether it was Prabhjot or Aisha who went out.

They needed a majority of five votes out of the total eight to be certain. But Sulochana outdid herself, and when Pepe read out the final tally—all the votes but her own going against Prabhjot—Prabhjot shook and screamed in fury. Her ire was directed mainly at Percy. 'You son of a bitch, what did you tell me? You said Aisha was going. Then you yourself vote against me? I know no one else liked my being here, but I thought we were friends, Percy.'

Percy's wan smile only infuriated her further.

'No one should believe this Percy, the traitor!' she yelled, addressing the rest. 'He's always up to tricks, playing one against the other. Throw him out. Beware of him, Mohinder, believe me. He won't spare anyone, his friend or captain or anyone. Just because Aisha looks good, he sides with her, the—'

Her expletive-laced tirade went on until finally Pepe had to step in. 'That's enough, Prabhjot. Shake hands with everyone and leave.'

Now that they had reached the halfway stage, with only seven of the original fourteen left in the fray, Pepe announced that it did not make sense to have teams competing any more. 'A team size of four or three or fewer is not effective. So now we disband the teams. Say goodbye to "The Black Mambas" and "The Crouching Tigers". From now, you will perform as individuals, competing against each other.'

'So who remains immune then, after a task?' Sufi asked. 'Only the winner?'

'The winner for sure. Or maybe the first two. Or some such rule,' Pepe said, 'that I will make clear just before the task. The rules can change for each task, but essentially, there will be one or more immune positions that you have to fight for. Clear?'

'Yes, sir.'

'Good. From tomorrow, it's every man, or woman, for himself, or herself.'

Reclining in his chair in the studio after reviewing the shoot, Pepe gazed at the ceiling with a sense of satisfaction. If he had not given Percy and Sulochana a second chance that day, Rohit and Prabhjot might still be on the show. Beyond that, he would not intervene in how they played their games. So any decision of his could impact anyone in *The Real Deal*, in a positive way for some, and badly for someone else. They played by his rules, and he could change the rules when he wanted to. He could sit back in his chair and watch the world of his creation unfold before him, sometimes playing out to his expectations, and sometimes surprising even him. Was that how God felt?

CHAPTER 13

Video Diary: Mohinder

I am a simple guy. So I like it when things are kept simple. That's why I liked Pepe sir's decision to get rid of the teams and make it an individual game from now on. No more team strategies, no more being pulled back by weaker guys in your team, no more having to play nice and polite because of the girls, and best of all, no more team politics.

I hate politics. I like it better now because the tasks are straightforward and fair: guys against guys, girls against girls. You do your task well, you perform and win, and you are safe. You vote out people you don't want on the show. This is how it should have been from the beginning.

Because then only the deserving would stay. So who do I think are the 'deserving' people? Rohit...well, let's not talk about Rohit any more because it still makes my blood boil to remember how he was sent out. Right now, the only good performers left are Sufi and myself. Percy is kind of average, but he tries hard. Irfan is useless.

The girls? I don't like girls. Don't get me wrong! I am a normal guy who loves looking at beautiful girls...but not here on *The Real Deal*. What are they doing here, apart from adding glamour? What is Aisha doing here, tell me that? She won't do a task if it messes her make-up and hairstyle. Okay, Sulochana can ride a bike, and I appreciate that, but that's it.

You can't really fight in a task against girls, you can't shout at them because if they burst into tears, you are the villain. I say, keep the girls out of this, and let the men fight it out among themselves. Or let them have a girls-only competition separately. But don't mix the two. I hope Pepe sir does not mind my advice. I am just being honest and open because that's my nature.

You can't be friends with a girl the natural way you can be with a guy. Like I can trust Percy and he can trust me. That's why I like him better than Sufi though I know Sufi is the better performer.

I will tell you why I don't like Sufi. Mr Sufi comes to me after the last task, before the vote-out. Wants my help in voting Percy out. I tell him straight out: 'Sorry mister, Percy is my buddy, and I will not vote against him for no reason.'

Well, actually, I know the reason and that's what makes me mad. It's all over a girl! Come on, you come all the way, get selected in *The Real Deal*, and then fight over a girl. Can't you do that outside? People think I am dumb, all Jat muscle and no brains, but they don't know me. I can observe and understand.

Percy has a crush on Sulochana. He won't admit it but it's so obvious. I have seen him many a time trying to talk to her alone. If we needed to convey anything to 'The Crouching Tigers', Percy is the first to volunteer and he always catches Sulochana for that.

But Sulochana and Sufi are far closer. In the swimming pool task, she was almost falling over him. You should have seen the look on Percy's face. Poor guy took it hard.

Sulochana is a foxy girl. She talks to both Sufi and Percy and encourages both. Even if I told Percy that, he would not understand me. Well, he will learn the hard way that this type of girl always goes for looks and money. She doesn't look at a guy's heart.

So I told Mr Ladykiller Sufi to focus on his tasks instead of chasing girls. And that I would vote Irfan out, who is even worse because all he does is to talk to girls or talk about them. At least Sufi does well in his tasks. But I would never betray a friend like Percy over a girl who does not care for anyone. Beating someone fair and square in a task is one thing; plotting behind their backs and betraying someone's trust is another.

What do I want? To win, of course, like everybody else. On my first attempt, I made it to the GD. The second time, I reached the personal interview level. And finally, the third time, up to here. When you come so close, you want to go all the way. Even if I go out now, I will still get one lakh. But it's not just the money any more.

I have nothing to fear from Percy or any of the girls. I can beat them all, any day, any task. It's only Sufi I have to watch out for. I need to catch him in a non-immune situation. And then, if Percy can somehow convince Sulochana to vote against Sufi, he will have three votes against him. I can count on Percy but can he count on Sulochana? It will be a good test whether she goes against Sufi, and perhaps the result will open Percy's eyes to the truth.

CHAPTER 14

E ver since that frightening encounter close-up with Pepe, Paras had imagined Pepe watching him all the time. Every step he took, every move he made, every conversation he had with Sulochana, he felt Pepe's eyes following him.

He tried to discern a deeper meaning behind Pepe's unnerving gaze, but that cold look, when not concealed behind his Aviator sunglasses, had always been a part of his persona. No, he could not really make out any difference in the manner Pepe treated Sulochana and himself, and the rest.

Paras breathed a little easier now that his worst nightmare—Pepe denouncing both of them in front of everybody, packing them off home amid a send-off of derisive hoots—was not coming true. If at all, Pepe, through his neutrality, was telling him something: that he would keep his end of the deal if Paras kept his.

And that realization was what had prompted Paras to go for it, plotting the ouster of Rohit with Sulochana, in front of the camera, of course. His original objective was being credited for the act of sending out the hottest contender on the show. While that would not be necessarily popular, it would catapult him to the forefront of everyone's attention, and perhaps, even win him a few supporters through his bravado.

Though he had cautioned Sulo not to reveal that it was his initiative to target Rohit, he knew it would not be difficult to trace the idea back to him, were anyone so inclined.

But then things had worked out, or fallen into place, in so unbelievable a fashion that he had been able to misdirect and deflect the blame first towards the hapless Chetan and then on to Prabhjot, such that his own hand was never seen. Prabhjot herself falsely attributing his duplicity to his feelings towards Aisha completed the confusion. He could not have come up with a better diversion even if he had wanted to. Sulochana could not keep a disbelieving smirk off her face on hearing Prabhjot's accusation.

Aisha's reaction topped the day for him. She was surprised, and then flattered to learn from Prabhjot's foul-mouthed farewell that Paras had betrayed her in order to save her, Aisha. She rewarded Paras with a bemused smile, and even spoke to him in hushed, softer tones for the next two days. Her whole demeanour seemed to suggest she was thankful to him for his act, but to be honest, her beauty demanded that kind of tribute.

Later on, watching Mohinder's fierce reaction, Paras was relieved to be on the right side of a strong guy like him, especially when there was no team structure left to count on for support. He was glad no one suspected him.

No one, that is, but for Sufi, who confronted him the next day. 'I knew you did something to Rohit.'

'Me? Why would I? He was my captain!'

'Didn't Prabhjot say you betrayed your captain?'

'She said many crazy things. According to her, I did all that for Aisha.'

'How does Aisha come into this?'

'Ask Prabhjot. Oh I am sorry, she's out, isn't it?' Paras laughed into Sufi's face. He was sure Sufi had only a hunch and no proof to back his suspicion.

'You may fool others, Percy, but you can't fool me.'

Paras could see the funny side of the situation—Sufi was as suspicious about Sulo and him as he was about Sufi and Sulo. He was certain Sufi would have noticed his private conversations with Sulo on more than one occasion, given the frequency with which they sought meetings to discuss how they were doing, or who they wanted to be voted out. In the beginning, Paras did try to ensure that Sufi was unaware of these meetings, but soon decided it was not worth the effort. He let Sulo handle Sufi's suspicions as she thought best.

Apparently, Sulo told Sufi that she could not help it if Paras sought her out to talk. She could not help it either, she said with a nonchalant shrug, if he found her attractive. But if Sufi just thought over it sensibly, wouldn't it be useful for him to know what the other team or the other guys were thinking or plotting? Sulo perhaps partially succeeded in allaying Sufi's suspicions, just as she only partially succeeded in convincing Paras that her interaction with Sufi was above board throughout.

Sufi had tried to enlist Mohinder's help to send Paras out. But as Mohinder updated Paras later, he had sent Sufi packing. Paras had long since realized that physical skill and strength scored over cerebral achievements any day as far as Mohinder went. Those who did well in the physical tasks earned his respect. Proficiency in other aspects were a waste of time. Thus, his admiration and fierce loyalty towards Rohit. He respected Sufi too for his performance in the tasks, but that was offset by his popularity among the girls.

Rohit had been popular too, but the difference was that Rohit did not even try. Sufi, on the other hand, appeared to consciously develop his good relations with all the girls, irrespective of which team they were in. And that, to Mohinder, was an unpardonable sin. If you were good at tasks, then you made sure you did well in that direction. To waste time over impressing girls instead was unforgivable; it made a sissy out of a man. Real men were guys like Rohit. They did what they wanted without caring for the girls; the girls would follow automatically.

That also explained Mohinder's counter-suggestion to Sufi that they send Irfan out instead of Paras. 'Another ladies' man!' Mohinder's exasperation was evident. 'At least Sufi does well in tasks while having a good time with the girls, but this Irfan is girls and only girls all the time. Seriously, it sickens me just to look at him.'

Indeed, when he stopped to think about it, it was surprising that Irfan had lasted so long on the show. He seemed to have slipped in under everyone's radar. Irfan's nomination for the vote-out found unanimous approval from the girls, and along with Mohinder's and Paras's votes, his vote-out became a certainty. Perhaps Irfan himself had been expecting the axe to fall for a long time because he did not show any surprise or malice at the vote-out, and thus created a far better impression through his good humour that day than he had throughout his stay. He said he was glad he was going away with at least 10,000 in his pocket.

In contrast, Aisha's farewell was not a smooth affair. Again, it was Mohinder's idea to get rid of her. 'Sure she is beautiful, Percy, but what's the use? Does her beauty win us tasks? She's so busy worrying about her make-up and hairstyle and how good she is looking that she forgets about the task. Isn't it better if only we guys are left and play the real stuff. Agreed?'

Paras would rather have disagreed. If he had his way, he would have her stay on as long as possible. It would be child's play to put her out later whenever it became necessary. Right now, she was all on his side, and that meant one certain vote to count upon in the vote-outs. And, she was eye candy. With Sulochana spending a lot more time with Sufi than with him, it gave him some solace to be in Aisha's company instead.

But she was not worth standing up against Mohinder and risk losing his friendship. So he gave in to Mohinder, and after that, she did not stand a chance of surviving. Sulochana was more than eager to go along with the idea—sending out the most beautiful girl on the show while leaving her untouched was what she wanted. That would reduce the girls' competition to a straightforward race between her and Naureen.

His assent made it three votes against Aisha, despite Sufi's opposition. 'I think she's okay. They are ganging up against her because they are not comfortable with how out-of-depth she makes them feel. I think I will go against Percy,' Sufi told Sulo.

'But why?' Sulochana asked. 'Are you just interested in saving Aisha?'

'And why are you interested in saving Percy?'

'You know it's nothing like that. There won't be enough votes against him, so there's no use.'

'Look, let's vote the way we feel like. No need for a unanimous vote. Let the most undeserving guy or girl go.'

'Easy for you to say that. You are immune tonight.'

'You don't have to worry,' Sufi said. 'Nobody is voting against you.'

Sulo reported the entire conversation to Paras, who was not bothered. 'Three votes against Aisha for sure. The other votes, if divided, will still make Aisha go. So let Sufi vote against me. I will tell Aisha to vote against you, as if we have all decided to go against you. Okay? That way, even if Naureen goes against you or me, we still have two votes at most against us, but Aisha has three against her. Get me?'

And that was exactly how the vote-out unfolded. Naureen took Sufi's side and voted against Paras, while Aisha herself voted against Sulochana. When Pepe counted the votes aloud, a stunned Aisha burst into tears.

'I don't know what happened,' she sobbed, 'but I have never been so humiliated in my life. I don't want to talk to anyone, except you, Percy. You were my only true friend here.' She hugged Paras, who was unable to believe that she had still not been able to work out who had voted against her. But there was no point in disillusioning her at this stage. 'I will miss you too, Aisha,' he said, hugging her back. He would, indeed, in a funny way. All she could think of at this point was that she was being humiliated.

Paras turned around to catch Sulochana's reaction but she was busy staring hard at Naureen. He could guess what Sulochana was thinking: but for Naureen, she would be the undisputed queen of *The Real Deal*, Season 5.

CHAPTER 15

Video Diary: Sulochana

I am a happy person tonight. I have finally achieved something I knew I was capable of. I am the best among girls, and as good as, if not better, than the guys. So what if no girl has ever won *The Real Deal* before? My father always knew my potential, even when I doubted myself. He would not be surprised to know that I am the last girl left in the show and only three guys remain as my competitors. He always said, 'You are in no way less than any boy.' Thank you, Papa, for believing in me.

Naureen was good. The other girls like Aisha or Sheetal had no business even being on the show. Now that Naureen is not here any more, I can appreciate her qualities: she was calm and confident and dignified. She had class. But it was because of her sense of dignity that she lost ultimately. She was not as desperate as I was in the swimming pool tug-of-war task.

Once I slipped, she should have pulled harder instead of giving me a few seconds to recover. If I was in her place, I would not have done that. And I didn't when she lost her footing. Someone has to win.

Percy backed me—well, he had to, given the number of times I have saved his ass from Sufi—and it was 'Well played but goodbye, Naureen'. Sufi, of course, did not like it one bit. I wish Paras, I mean Percy, and Sufi would become friends instead of being at each other's throats all the time. I am friends with both, so it puts me in a difficult position. Mohinder, I don't care about. He doesn't talk to me much, and I am fine keeping my distance from him.

I wish I were not drawn into their stupid politics and vote-outs. They would enjoy the show more if they had the time or sense to appreciate the scenery and places we go through. Wasn't Gwalior Fort amazing? But no, Sufi and Percy are talking to me, and not looking at each other. And I am like, will the both of you just shut up and let me take in the lovely views around?

Percy and I relate to each other because we both have a similar small-town background. We know how it feels to come from a tiny place and compete with the metro guys and girls. We are both not that fluent in English, but that does not mean we are less capable.

Initially, I had the impression that the metro people would be so smart and clever that I would feel totally ignorant before them. But soon I came to realize that under the skin we are all the same.

Actually, it was Sufi who helped me understand that. Sufi is different, you know. No one is more metro than Sufi, but he can still put himself in my shoes. He says the only difference between us is that he grew up in a big city and was sent to posh schools that charge exorbitant fees. His parents are hotshot people in Delhi, but you would never know that by talking to him...he is so down to earth. He can appreciate the value of money, and that he was lucky to be born where he was. I think it is an amazing quality to know your real self.

Take yesterday's incident. We took a break during the journey to lunch at a dhaba. A ten- or twelve-year-old boy was cleaning the tables. It made Sufi sad. He talked about the boy's lost childhood, of how he would never have anything to look back upon fondly on growing up. Percy laughed at that. The boy, he said, did not have time to have fond memories. He had to play with the cards he was dealt, that's all. And Percy said he wondered why only the rich felt guilty and sorry about others' poverty, obviously pointing at Sufi.

I suppose Percy is right in a practical sense, and Sufi is idealistic and sensitive, but the difference in their views really struck me at that time.

Sufi has class. Real class shows in your manners, in your speech. You don't talk or show off about how cool you are. How classy is that, tell me? Wish Percy could understand that. But Percy is always trying to warn me about how bad Sufi is. He is mistaken but he will not listen to me, so I have stopped trying to convince him that Sufi is actually a nice guy. You just have to approach him in the right way.

Sometimes, nowadays, I wish there did not have to be only one winner. If there was some way Sufi and Percy and I could all be declared winners in the end...that would be ideal. Yes, I know we are all here to win, but life isn't always about winning and losing because there are some things more precious. Life is complicated. You have to make choices. But if all the choices you face are between good and bad, or right and wrong, then life would be easy, wouldn't it?

Oh God, I have never talked two lines about life before! Do I sound philosophical? If someone had mentioned my name and philosophy in the same sentence before, I would have laughed. But after coming here, after talking to others especially Sufi, I feel I have been thinking a lot more, asking more questions of myself. I did not have this sense of self-awareness before. I did not even know what self-awareness meant. I suddenly feel so mature. Thank you, *Real Deal.*

Okay, I was just kidding about sharing the trophy. I want to be the sole and ultimate winner of *The Real Deal,* Season 5, and leave the guys far behind. That is Sulo for you, the first ever *Real Deal* girl champion.

CHAPTER 16

Naureen's unceremonious exit thrilled Sulochana and enraged Sufi. 'We have to be united, Sulo, don't you see? We need to vote together to be effective. See how Percy and Mohinder decide and vote together? That's how they voted Naureen out and that's why we need to get together so that we vote out whom we want.'

'I thought you said a little while back that we are teams no more. We vote as individuals,' Sulochana said.

'But those guys are still voting as a team. That puts us at a disadvantage,' Sufi said, his frustration evident. 'Today it is in your favour, tomorrow it won't be.'

'I don't understand why you are so dejected to see Naureen go. Would you rather have seen me out instead?'

'You were immune, so you were in no danger anyway. I would rather see Percy out. Mohinder is okay; he is a good performer.'

'Plus the fact that he was immune too.'

'All right, fair enough. The next task I will win and then we will see who is immune and who goes out. If I win, will you go along with me and vote as I say?'

'Win the task first,' Sulo said, a bit curtly.

Sufi appeared to have taken the line to heart because he was charged up on the eve of the next task. And when Pepe announced that it was a water task again, he flashed Sulochana a grin, because water was his element. The task was to search for objects in a pond. The pond was natural and shallow, up to Sufi's waist and Paras's abdomen at its deepest point in the centre. The water was a little murky—not as clear as that in a swimming pool, but neither as opaque green as an algae-covered pond.

They would have to go underwater to seek the bright yellow balls, as the bottom was not visible from above the surface. The objective was straightforward: whoever found the most balls in the allotted time was the winner and earned the coveted immunity. Swimming goggles would help them keep their eyes open underwater.

The huge advantage Sufi had over the others was that he could swim underwater for longer. The rest had to surface every now and then to take a fresh breath and duck their heads in again in order to resume their search. Sufi, on the other hand, could look around for a much longer time without a break. Even if someone else located a ball, he could swim towards it faster than the other person could wade across.

Within the first few minutes, it was clear that the task was a no-contest. The number of balls Sufi gathered was more than what all the others combined had collected.

'Told you,' Sufi whispered to Sulochana. 'Sulo, we agreed. I want Percy out. Two of us means two votes against him. If I can convince Mohinder that will confirm it.'

'Mohinder won't vote against Percy,' Sulochana said. 'But he will against me.'

'Fine. If Percy votes against Mohinder, that will still mean two votes against Percy, one against you, and one against Mohinder. So Percy still goes out.'

'What if Percy votes against me?' Sulochana asked. 'Then it is two each against Percy and me.'

'Oh, he won't go against you. He is your big admirer, isn't he?' Sufi chuckled at the predicament Paras would find himself in. 'You will see for yourself what kind of person he is tonight. But let me try to convince Mohinder first so that there's no danger of a tie.'

Later that evening, Mohinder greeted Paras with a thump on the back. 'So buddy, your friend Mr Sufi has not given up trying to send you out. He and the girl you like are going to vote against you.'

'Who told you that?'

'Sufi. He wants my vote against you too, to make sure. The bugger has been trying hard to get you out for the last two vote-outs. What did you do to make him your enemy?'

'Nothing. Maybe he doesn't like my face. Or he just cannot accept the fact that a boy from an unknown place, who cannot speak good English, has made it as far as him.'

'Or, that Sulochana talks to you too. I think it's more to do with the girl,' Mohinder said thoughtfully.

'Maybe. So what are you going to do?'

'Would I have told you all this if I was going to vote against you? Fuck Sufi. I told you before, our friendship comes first. What we can do is that both of us go against Sulochana.'

'Sulochana?'

'No other option. I want to vote against Sufi, but he is bloody immune. Both Sufi and Sulochana against you makes it two against you. We counter that with two against Sulochana. Then we go to a tiebreak and hopefully you will beat her.'

'But—'

'This is the best we can do. If our votes get split, you will go out. Don't you see that?'

'I see now,' Paras said, hearing his own voice go husky.

'In a way, it's good. It will leave just us three guys, and then let the best man win. Having a girl in it complicates stuff. You just focus on how you come out the winner in the tiebreaker.'

'Sulo, Mohinder says I should vote against you.'

'Sufi says I should vote against you.'

'I know. That's why I have to vote against you.'

'You have to, Paras?'

'I have to, if you have to. But the thing is, we don't have to.'

'How?'

'Listen.'

At the vote-out, Sufi looked the most relaxed, understandably so because of his immunity. Mohinder's expression said he could not care less about the whole affair and it was all a waste of time as far as he was concerned. Paras glanced at Sulochana and sensed she was feeling as tense as him.

Pepe stepped out from the shadows, rubbing his hands together in glee in anticipation of the vote-out. 'Well, well. From fourteen to four, and in another few minutes, only three. So who thinks he or she is going out?'

Both Paras and Sulochana raised their hands.

'Oh, don't worry,' Pepe said, 'only one goes out at a time, not two. And whoever goes takes away at least one lakh rupees. Not bad, eh?'

'Not at all, sir,' Paras said.

'All right, folks, business time. Step to the table and cast your votes. Remember Sufi is immune, so no vote can go against him.'

All of them trooped one by one to the table and wrote their chosen name on the voting paper. Paras imagined this scene, when shown on TV later, would be in slow motion, accompanied by suspense-inducing drum beats, and interspersed by at least two commercial breaks. Now, of course, it was a rather drab and silent process.

Pepe took the four cards and began to read the names aloud.

'Percy.'

Sufi smirked.

'Expecting this?' Pepe asked.

'Yes, sir,' Paras said.

'Sulochana.'

Mohinder smirked.

'Expecting this?'

'Yes, sir.'

Pepe continued, 'Mohinder.'

Paras and Sulochana stared fixedly at the ground.

'Expecting this?'

'No, sir.' Mohinder glared at Sufi, who shook his head.

'Mohinder. Second vote. You are out.'

A shocked silence of a few seconds followed, broken only by Sufi's sharp audible intake of breath.

'No, no, sir, there's a mistake.' Paras cringed to hear Mohinder's subdued voice. He didn't want to see a snivelling, crestfallen Mohinder. He ought to go out roaring and storming.

'Yes, I see you were not expecting it. But I am sorry, there's no mistake.' Pepe's voice was flat. 'I think I can count four votes. See here: two to you, one to Percy, and one to Sulochana.'

'It wasn't me, Mohinder,' Sufi said.

After a few more painful silent seconds, which Paras wished would get over quickly, Mohinder asked, 'Percy?'

Paras kept his eyes fixed on the ground.

'Sufi, beware of this guy and the girl,' Mohinder said. 'They have an understanding. They have fucked me, they will fuck you too.'

'What are you talking about?' Sulochana yelled at him. 'What happened here was completely fair. You were not immune and one of us had to go. You are going, that's all. Totally according to the rules. Ask Pepe if you like.'

'She's right,' Pepe said, shrugging his shoulders. 'Nothing against the rules.'

'What did you do this for, Percy?' Paras wished Mohinder would rage and shout instead of whimpering like a stray puppy kicked aside. 'For a mere girl, you betrayed a friend? Someone who saved you at least two times in the vote-outs, and God knows how many times in the tasks? Why, Percy, why? Do you think you can look at a mirror and face yourself?'

Paras looked up and stared Mohinder squarely in his face. 'I don't know what you are talking about. I look into a mirror only to comb my hair and while shaving. I don't talk to my reflection.'

CHAPTER 17

Video Diary: Sufi

I won my task today. I was immune. I am one of the final three left in the competition. So I should be happy, shouldn't I?

I don't know what happened there today. I don't know if I am more shocked or surprised or angry or betrayed or just sad. I am not sad because Mohinder is gone. I was never a close friend of his. Just had a healthy respect for him as an opponent. I am angry because the person who most deserved to be kicked out is still here while a true performer has to go home. You know who I am talking about. Percy. I have never made a secret of my opinion about him.

The moment I knew it was an underwater task, I knew I would win. Not a boast, but water is my playground. I learned swimming at the age of eight. I have won competitions at school and college. And the others barely know swimming. So it was child's play for me to beat them. Until that point, everything was fine. But something must have happened between then and the vote-out.

Oh, all right, who am I fooling? 'Something' must have happened! Of course I know what happened. Percy and Sulo got together and voted against Mohinder. There is no other explanation. Mohinder was right.

You should have seen Mohi's face after Pepe said he was out. He understood immediately that he had been betrayed by his great friend Percy. Well, then he should have listened to me. I had warned him about trusting Percy, and now see what happened.

But I feel betrayed too. By Sulo. If I had warned Mohi about Percy two or three times, I must have warned Sulo a hundred times. Percy is a cheat, disloyal, dishonest, liar and a non-performer to boot, who has reached this point only by hiding behind someone popular like Rohit or by playing dirty politics. How can anyone else not see through him? He is a bloody fake. His very name is fake: Paras, not Percy. How do you trust a guy who cannot even stick to the name his parents gave him?

I just do not understand what kind of hold he has on Sulo. It is just her good nature that she cannot hear anything negative about anyone. She tries defending Percy's actions to me. That's so ridiculous. Why? Just because both are from small towns in Uttar Pradesh they feel some sort of kinship?

But Sulo ought to know that I have never looked down upon her in any way. She's a great girl. I love her attitude. She rides a bike better than most guys. I liked having her on my team, and even if she's a competitor now, that does not change my opinion.

And then it strikes you that Percy is also a competitor. Come on, man, he should not even be on the show. He should just be watching it on TV. That's his level; that's what he is capable of. Not a single redeeming feature. Maybe I am overreacting but something about him just irritates me beyond words. His manner of speaking, or body language, or something. Rohit or Mohinder should have been in the top three, not Percy.

Poor Mohi. What's the point of shouting now that Percy is a traitor? I already knew that. He said Sulo and Percy would get together and stab me in the back too, but I cannot believe that of Sulo. She is probably already regretting what she has done. But of Percy, I can believe anything. He can stoop to any level. He must have thought of that 'mirror' dialogue a week before.

Anyway, what's done is done. What I have to do now is crystal clear. Percy or Sulo or myself. Who do you think I want should go out next?

CHAPTER 18

If Sufi were a cartoon character, he would have columns of steam billowing out of his ears. But as he confronted Sulochana immediately after Mohinder's vote-out, she found nothing comic about him.

'What's the big deal, Sufi?' Sulochana asked. 'It's not as if I voted against you. I didn't know Mohinder was your best friend that you should get so upset.'

'It's not that, Sulo, you know.'

'Then what is it?' she asked, knowing only too well the reason he was worked up.

'We agreed. That you would do what I wanted if I won the task. And I asked you to vote against Percy, but you did not. Instead, you go with him and vote against Mohinder.'

'So?'

'So I don't know if I can trust you any more, Sulo,' he said, flinging his arms up in despair. 'If I had not been immune, who knows, you both might have voted against me? I don't know what power this Percy has over you.'

'Nonsense.'

'Is it? You guys seem to have a secret understanding. That's what Mohinder said. That's what happened during Naureen's vote-out too.'

'Sufi, you should be glad Mohinder is out. He was your biggest rival. Who would you rather face off in a task: Mohinder or Percy?'

'Percy, of course. Anyone can beat him,' Sufi said, smirking.

'Well then, you should be thanking me. You have a much better chance of winning among the three of us. Don't you agree?'

'Maybe.'

Sulochana saw she had tickled his vanity. 'Aw, don't be so modest, Sufi. I know it, you are the best.'

'Well, I don't deny I have a good chance to win. But Sulo, I need your support. And then when I see you side with Percy and not me, it hurts. For me, it is the same whether you win or I win.'

'Really?'

'Of course. You are not just my best friend here, Sulo. You get me?' he asked, looking at her anxiously.

'No, I don't get it,' Sulo said. 'Tell me loud and clear.'

Paras could not have accosted her at a worse time than just after Sufi had finished talking to her. Though he usually turned sour upon finding her with Sufi, this time he continued to look smug. 'So what was Sufi complaining about? My still being on the show?'

'Not really.'

'Three times he has tried to send me out and failed each time. He must be frustrated.'

'While you seem very happy,' Sulochana said. 'I thought you would be a little down after voting Mohinder out. He was your best friend.'

'Oh, come on, Sulo,' Paras snapped, losing his smile finally. 'What does a best friend mean here? We are all here to win, aren't we? Would it have made you happier instead if I had sacrificed myself for the sake of our six-week-long friendship?'

She had not meant that but she was relieved to see Paras shed his cheer. If she was feeling confused, he did not have any right to look so pleased with the world.

'He should have known blind trust goes only so far on this show. It's his fault for not looking out,' Paras said.

She had meant that he could perhaps show a little sympathy to the guy who had given him his unflinching support, or at least, not mock him on top of betraying him. But if Paras could not understand that, then there was no point in trying to explain to him how he ought to feel.

'True, his fault for being trusting. I guess then you should not trust me, nor I you.'

'What nonsense you come up with! Our case is different.'

'Is it really?'

Paras stared hard at her, his eyebrows marking furrows in his forehead. She knew he was bursting with doubts, questions and accusations, none of which he could dare voice. Ever since Pepe had given them the almighty scare and come within a whisker of throwing them out of the show, both had scrupulously avoided talking in the absence of cameras. At most, Paras would throw her a meaningful glance or suggest something with a nod or shake of his head. With the camera eye and the microphone ears keeping track, they had to be careful not to mention anything about their past, though they could do their plotting without inhibition.

'You have changed.' Paras's voice was flat, as if making a pronouncement. 'Does Sufi have something to do with this?'

It was all she could do to stop herself from rolling her eyes. When would he grow up? 'Did I say anything about Sufi?'

'Then why are you doubtful? What does that show-off really mean to you?'

'He is not a show-off.'

'You really have changed,' Paras repeated, not taking his eyes off her for a second.

'I haven't changed, Paras. But times change.'

Later that night, alone in her room, now that she was the only girl on the show, Sulochana wished she could take back that last statement. The instant she had made it, Paras's face fell like a curtain covering a lighted window. He would have wanted to say a lot more, perhaps remind her once again—as though she needed any reminding—of all the things he had done for her since the Bisalpur days, but this time he preferred, or was forced, to let his injured expression do the talking for him.

How she owed her very presence on the show to his idea, advice, support and encouragement. And it was true, every bit of it, that without Paras she would be in Bisalpur, trying in despair to cope with the studies she hated only in order to escape the fate of being married off to some stranger.

But hadn't she repaid her debt yet? What was it, if not debt, that compelled her to support him in every vote-out and go against Sufi? Wasn't that good enough to compensate for all that he had done for her? But again, surely it wasn't mere obligation that tied her to Paras? What about the times they spent together in Bisalpur, bike-riding or at the cinemas, or the shared ice creams at Bisalpur Palace? Or how about that evening at Gajanan's flat in Delhi when they almost made love for the first and the only time? No, it could not be only gratitude that tied her to him. Or had that aborted lovemaking itself been a result of the gratitude? Could she ever truly see Paras outside this miasmic cloud of debt, obligation and gratitude?

What, on the other hand, did she owe Sufi? What had he done for her that she should side with him, which meant going against Paras and sending out the very guy who had got her into the show in the first place? She could not imagine a more ironic act of betrayal. But these feelings—gratitude and betrayal—had no place in a relationship or on the show either, as Paras did not forget reminding her. Did gratitude come with an expiry date, or was it supposed to last lifelong? Or did it depend on the nature of the favour?

What she felt for Sufi, or Sufi for her, was thankfully bereft of these guilt-inducing feelings. When Sufi told her that she was not just his best friend, and she asked him to elaborate on the subject, he had done so. He had obeyed her, unmindful of the presence of the cameramen, and the episode director, whose expression clearly indicated that he had hit a jackpot with this display of raw emotion. Paras, on the other hand, was always extra-cautious about the presence of the cameras, and calibrated what and how much he said to her depending on it. Perhaps she ought to stop weighing Sufi on the one hand and Paras on the other.

Sufi told her that he had thought of her as someone special the moment he first saw her in the Delhi auditions. At that point, he had no inkling of his making it to the show, leave alone her qualification. He was taken aback when she attacked him during the group discussion, but he did not hold that against her because he realized she was only trying to get the moderator's attention. Indeed, he could not hold anything she did against her.

Imagine his joy when he saw her next in Mumbai at the kick-off episode of the show, and then, to top it, when she became a member of 'The Crouching Tigers' under his captaincy. It was as though a script written especially for him was being played out. Didn't it all point to destiny, fate? He normally did not go for that kind of fairy-tale stuff, but his world had changed after meeting her.

Of course she was beautiful, but that was only one among the numerous aspects of her that fascinated him. He liked her spunk, her attitude...her attitude was her biggest asset, if she didn't know it already. As far as he was concerned, she was the one who possessed the true *Real Deal* spirit, and not Rohit or Naureen or he himself. Yes, he was serious. Her biggest accomplishment was overcoming her handicap of not hailing from a metro, and not merely competing, but surpassing other big-city contenders. He knew it was not a trivial disadvantage. Others gang up easily against someone they consider an outsider, different from them, but she did not let that happen. Her English might not be her strong point, but she did not let that hold her back. That required guts.

No, he didn't laugh at her howlers. The others had studied in English-medium schools, talked frequently in English at home and with friends, and watched English movies and TV serials. So what was the big deal in their speaking in English?

And then, she won everyone over by her daredevilry in riding the bike. If that was not the *Real Deal* spirit Pepe talked about, then he didn't know what was. She was as deserving a winner of the competition as he was. In fact, he did not see any difference between his winning or hers, because he thought of them together as one unit. 'Whether I win or you win, it means we win, Sulo. Because I see us together even outside and after the show, and that is because I love you, Sulo.'

His serious manner of speaking and his flushed face had given her a hint of what his speech was leading to, but even as it reached the climax, she quivered with pleasure on hearing him out. Paras was incapable of such feeling. He liked her, she knew, but to express himself in such a romantic fashion was beyond him. But again, she was comparing them. The episode director, meanwhile, hovering behind the camera, could not hide his grin at this drama playing out before him.

The only certainty in Sulochana's mind was that no matter what happened in the next task, she would make it to the finals. If she won, she was immune. If either Paras or Sufi won, he would make sure she stayed and the other guy went out. She only hoped that she would not have to decide between them, for she truly did not know who she would choose. She hid her predicament in her video diary. She felt that everyone who watched the show would root for her going with Sufi.

No one knew and could understand her bond with Paras. She glossed over her confusion by giggling at the camera: 'I hope I don't have to decide who goes and who stays because I hate hurting anyone.'

Another point Sulochana had a strong inkling about was that whatever the task they would be set would not be a test of physical strength. Her being the sole girl left in the fray would ensure that there would be no hauling buckets of water or rolling logs or mud-wrestling involved. Most probably, they would come up with some mind game or treasure hunt to decide the finalists. No wonder few girls survived towards the end of the show. Mind games did not look as exciting on TV as the ones involving sweat and blood and blows and tears. Her presence on the show at these final stages was a huge achievement, and she was bound to leave with at least two lakh rupees in her kitty. Wouldn't her father have been proud of her? She wished he could see her now from wherever he was, even if it was for just a moment.

But why was she even worrying about the task? No matter what, she would make it to the finals, which meant four lakhs and not just two. The ones who ought to be worrying were the guys. She wondered how they were getting along, now that they were forced to share a room.

In a rare display of solidarity, both Paras and Sufi had requested Pepe that they be put up in separate rooms, since it was no secret that each could not stand the sight of the other. It was a given that they were not going to communicate or plan anything together, so there was no point in sharing a room.

Pepe rejected their request peremptorily. Just because they could not stand each other did not mean that YTV would bear the unnecessary expense of renting another room. Let them take the task of tolerating each other's presence as another challenge of *The Real Deal*. This was not the place to act like prima donnas.

Their mutual loathing did not let them stay in their room together for more than a few minutes. Each came to Sulochana separately and complained how the other was utterly impossible to get along with. Sulochana was glad she had her room all to herself. She was patient with them on their first two visits, but the third time Paras knocked on her door, she turned him back. 'No, there's nothing to talk about now. I need to rest.' Showing off for the camera, she rolled her eyes and sighed, 'Guys!'

The next morning, after bolting down their breakfast, they assembled in front of the guest house they were put up at, as instructed by Pepe. There, after much ado about how momentous this task was, as it would decide the finalists, Pepe eventually revealed that the task was indeed a treasure hunt. Sulochana concealed a yawn.

'All right, folks. We are in this small town of Chhata, which I am sure none of you have heard of before, and thus know nothing about. Am I correct?'

'We are somewhere near Mathura and Vrindavan,' Sufi said, 'but that's all I know.'

'Good. Because for this task you will have to find out all about this town as quickly as possible. Its history, its streets, main roads, buildings, popular shops and so on. There will be clues to lead you from one place to the next. The clues will be written on a piece of paper, and that paper will be with someone at the place the clue leads to. That someone could be a watchman, a shopkeeper, a beggar or anyone, but he won't be wearing a *Real Deal* T-shirt, so you'll have to figure out who it is, and get the clue from him or her. Get me?'

'Yes, Pepe.'

Pepe nodded, and continued. 'The final treasure is a miniature of *The Real Deal* trophy. You have to get that and return here. The one who gets here first is the winner of this task and becomes immune. He, or she, therefore automatically qualifies for the finals that will crown *The Real Deal* winner. So are all of you looking forward to this penultimate task, or rather, ultimate for one of you?'

'Yes, Pepe. But how do we get around the town? Walking?' Sufi asked.

'Why? Have you forgotten your Hunks? You can use them to get around. Sulochana, I don't need to ask you this, but it's my duty to. If you are not comfortable riding the bike, one of the crew can drive you around. But he will act strictly as a driver, and will not assist you in solving or finding the clues in any way. In fact, not just Sulochana, you guys too can opt for a driver so that you can focus only on the clues.'

'No, we don't need anyone to drive us around.' The reaction from the three was unanimous.

'All right, folks, get going then,' Pepe said. 'There's no time limit, but try to return before sunset! Our clueholders are not going to remain at their places all day and night. And, just one warning. We have planted wrong or misleading clues too. So look out for red herrings.'

'Red herrings? What does that mean?' Paras asked.

Sufi chuckled. 'False or misleading clues. That's what Pepe said now.'

'I asked Pepe, not you.'

'Guys, no bickering. Go to your bikes now. Run.'

Despite the exhortation from Pepe to infuse urgency and zest into the task, Sulochana felt strangely unmoved, almost stoical. She realized that because she was not tense at the prospect of losing in the task and forgoing immunity, she was enjoying it all the more. A sense of calm pervaded her and ironically, she felt mentally quicker and in control, because there was nothing or no one rushing her. Where she would have earlier merely tagged along with Sufi or Paras, content to follow their lead, now when Pepe read out the first clue, 'Get moving, time flies quickly', she waited. While Sufi and Paras ran to their bikes, gunned them to life and sped away, she mulled over the clue before starting her bike, undaunted by the lead the guys were gaining. She knew it was more important to crack the clue first rather than diving headfirst into a wild goose chase.

'Time' obviously was the keyword, probably indicating a clock tower in the town. But the clue could not be so obvious; it could be one of the red herrings Pepe had cautioned about. Two minutes after Sufi's and Paras's departure, Sulochana drove out sedately onto the main road, taking in the relatively bigger-looking buildings and shops on the way. She asked a passerby if there was a clock tower in the town. He pointed her down the road.

Paras was present right at the foot of the clock tower and was not surprised to see her coast to a halt beside him. 'Sufi was here and has already left for some other place a minute back,' Paras said. 'But I don't think this is the right place. The man here has this—'

'Which man?' Sulochana asked.

'Oh, don't waste time. The man is not important. It's the clue he has: "Be brave; take the iron road". But there's no railway station or track near this town. I have asked five people already.'

'I don't think we should be discussing the clues.'

Paras shrugged. 'Pepe did not say anything against it.'

No, Pepe had not explicitly prohibited their talking, but it was obvious you could not collaborate on an individual task. All of a sudden, Sulochana remembered crossing a big watch-and-clock store about a kilometre back. She had wondered about the viability of setting up such a large store in a small town. Perhaps the 'time' in the first clue had something to do with that store. She swung her bike around as Paras asked, 'Where are you going? Did you get it? I have to win here, Sulo.'

Ignoring him, Sulochana roared back down the road. She knew he was desperate to win because if Sufi came first, it was as good as curtains for Paras. But that did not mean flouting the rules before the camera and risking Pepe's wrath again. He would not be as forgiving a second time. She looked at the rearview mirror and was thankful that Paras was not following her.

Her hunch about the watch store turned out to be correct. The second clue, which she got from the store owner, pointed her to the sole college in the town. Again, the clue was tantalizingly obvious but as she could not make a better guess, she followed it.

In this manner, Sulochana visited the Mahavir College, where the security guard at the entrance held the clue; the temple at the banks of the Sarayu river, where the temple priest had tucked the next clue in a fold of his dhoti; then back to the Kaka Halwai Sweet House in the main road, and so on.

Though she was stumped at a couple of places, she found it fun rushing here and there to different corners of the town, never pessimistic about her chances or questioning whether she was on the right track. Two of the crew dogged her journey, never letting her out of their sight. The town was even smaller than Bisalpur, and so it was no surprise to keep bumping into Sufi or Paras every now and then.

She was surprised Sufi had not already won. Instead, he wore a puzzled expression whenever she saw him. He acknowledged her with a brief, shy smile, probably embarrassed about his confession the previous evening. Paras, on the other hand (she was comparing again!), glared at her for not helping him out with the clues.

At one corner, she came across the two of them confronting each other. 'You have hidden a clue, haven't you?' She heard Sufi's angry accusation. 'There is something missing.'

'I don't know what you are talking about,' Paras said, protesting his innocence. He thumbed behind at the cameramen following him. 'These guys are watching me all the time.' Catching sight of her, he turned to ask, 'Is this guy crazy or something?'

'Look, Sulo, what he has done,' Sufi began, 'he—'

Sulochana cut them short. 'Sorry, whatever your quarrel is, keep me out of it.' She would not put it beyond Paras to scuttle Sufi's chances any way he could. But, as he said, every step of his was under scrutiny. But again, a missing link in the chain of clues would explain Sufi's unexpected struggle in the treasure hunt.

Whatever the case was, they could handle it without her intervention. So she went ahead, ignoring them, intent on following her lead.

Eventually, after stumbling through seven clues, Sulochana was taken aback when the security guard at the SBI ATM handed her the miniature *Real Deal* trophy, instead of the next clue, while grinning broadly at the camera.

It took her a few seconds to realize that this was her nightmare come true. She had not expected to win. She had been comfortably relaxed all through the hunt, happy to let Sufi or Paras overtake her and fight it out themselves. Ironically, it was her relaxed state of mind that enabled her to turn over the clues in her mind, decoding the real ones and discarding the red herrings. She had brought her dilemma on to herself.

Sulochana handed over the trophy to Pepe a few minutes later, torn by conflicting emotions. Winning a task on her own was something to be proud of; it meant she was immune and was through to the grand final, but it also meant she would now have to decide who to save—Sufi or Paras.

She was the winner; she was immune, as Pepe did not forget to remind her again, and not either of the guys. Hers would be the decisive vote because they were bound to vote against each other. Sufi and Paras joined her some time later after being informed that their treasure hunt was now futile. Both were painfully aware of the significance of her vote.

'Can I count on you, Sulo, this one time?' Sufi asked. 'This will be your most important decision in life, but I believe in you, because I know you are good and you will do what's good and fair. I don't want to talk about Percy because he is not important. Please keep in mind what I have told you before. My feelings don't end with this show.'

She was aware of Paras looking daggers at Sufi from a distance. Perhaps there was an unwritten guy code that forbade him to approach her when his rival was talking to her. Sufi would be expected to follow the same code when it was Paras's turn to try to win her favour.

'Yes, Sufi, I am with you,' Sulochana said.

As soon as a relieved Sufi left her alone, Paras was beside her. 'You are with me, Sulo, right? This is our last chance to put him out. Then you can forget all about him and his big-city show-off style. You should have helped me out today. Why didn't you?'

'How could I?'

'After...after...' Paras hesitated, glancing nervously at the camera, 'after everything I have done for you? You have nothing in common with Sufi. But we have...we have a lot in common. Remember. Have you forgotten everything?'

'No, I haven't. I am with you, Percy.'

CHAPTER 19

That night, after the final vote-out, Sulochana was prepared for a sleepless night, haunted by her momentous decision of that evening. But immediately after the vote-out, Pepe declared that all of them—both the finalists, as well as the entire crew that had toiled continually—deserved a break of one day when they would have to do absolutely nothing. Some other shows on other channels that considered themselves rivals of *The Real Deal*, said Pepe contemptuously, shot the final episode after a gap of a few months. They did this because they were scared someone would leak the final results to the public before the episode was aired. *The Real Deal* and the YTV channel did not have to resort to this trickery because they were a lot quicker and efficient in editing their footage and getting the episode on TV. And more important, they knew competitors could not work up the same momentum or enthusiasm in the show after such a long gap.

So when Sulochana was again alone in her room at night, she found that instead of worrying herself sick over her decision, or playing back the events of that evening in her mind endlessly, she was able to unwind. She could sleep as long as she wished because there would be no surprise knock at the door early in the morning to inform her of the task of the day.

What had happened, had happened. How she wished either Sufi or Paras had won the task, earned his immunity and thus taken the decision off her hands. But it was not to be, and if she was meant to take the hardest decision of her life, well, so be it.

One had to take the long-term view. In the short term, it hurt, just as it did now, like a thousand needles piercing her heart. But by the next morning, she knew, or hoped, that she would feel better. The next week would be even better, and by the next month or year, the details of this evening would grow fuzzy and vague, before fading away altogether. She had merely chosen the path that would hurt her less later on.

Before she could continue drawing this line of thought, she fell asleep but woke to an insistent knocking. It was 9 a.m., which meant she had had a long and restful sleep. Pepe had declared that no one would disturb them the whole day, so then who was it banging on her door? If it was a surprise task, she would throw it back in his face. She got off the bed and opened the door.

'Good morning, Sulo,' Paras greeted her with a smile as radiant as the sun.

'Good morning, Paras,' Sulochana said sleepily. 'How are you?'

Paras bounded into the room and leapt onto the bed. 'How am I? Sulo, just imagine, we are in the finals of *The Real Deal*! Does it make sense to you? The finals of *The Real Deal*! What would you have said four months ago in Bisalpur if I had told you we would be in this position today?'

For a moment, she was shocked when he mentioned Bisalpur before she remembered it was everybody's day off, including the crew's. 'That you are crazy, of course.' Sulochana had to smile.

'Now who's crazy, tell me?'

'Yes, you were right and I was wrong. Happy?'

'I am,' Paras said. 'You are happy too, right? You don't seem so excited.'

'Of course. I just woke up,' Sulochana said, quickly. 'Just that I am tired.'

'Oh, don't be...one more task, and then you can relax for as long as you wish.'

Sulochana nodded to show her agreement, but did not feel like prolonging the chatter. The sight of Paras was reminding her of things she would rather forget. She gazed at the bedspread while Paras tried to engage her attention.

'I...' Paras began, paused and then began again. 'I didn't thank you for the last night.'

'Well, don't,' Sulochana said, brusquely.

'Yes, but...to be frank, I was scared, Sulo. But I should not have been. I knew you would vote for me.'

'You knew?'

'Yes, you had to vote for me.'

'I had to?'

'Everything between us, I mean. That's why you had to. How could you have voted for him? I admit I was scared that you would, but I should have known better.'

'I didn't have to vote for you, Paras.'

'But you did.'

'Yes, I did, but I did not have to. Please understand the difference.'

She sensed his unspoken anger as it was his turn to stare at the bedspread while she looked out the window. What was the point in being harsh with him now that she had chosen him over Sufi? The deed was done. It was his sense of entitlement that angered her. Not only was she burdened by her own sense of obligation at every step, but Paras also expected her to keep paying her dues to him.

Her colluding with him instead of Sufi at every vote-out, his anger with her for not helping him out in the treasure hunt, and even this most difficult decision of her life favouring him, all were nothing but her repayment of the debt in instalments.

Yes, the deed was done, but she knew Paras was reliving last night's vote-out in his mind, as she was.

Though both Paras and Sufi had nonchalantly shrugged off Pepe's question whether they were scared of being voted out, the tension on both their faces was evident. Pepe laughed. 'Look at your faces, guys. They tell me a more truthful answer. But that's natural, and it's good that being here on *The Real Deal* means so much to you guys. It isn't just about the money. Right, guys?'

'Right.'

'Absolutely.'

'Great. This will be the last vote-out of this season as we won't have a vote-out in the finals obviously. I will keep it short and sweet. Just three votes. A straight battle between Percy and Sufi, as Sulochana is immune.

'Start voting. First Percy, followed by Sufi, and then Sulochana, because of course her vote will be the decisive one, unless one of you guys is thinking of sacrificing himself for the other. Is that the case?'

'No way.'

Pepe was evidently relishing this vote-out. 'So who will you choose, Sulochana?'

'It will be clear in a few minutes, won't it?'

'Sure, it will. But have you made your decision? Or are you going to toss a coin before voting?'

Sulochana laughed. 'No, I have made up my mind.'

Sufi and Paras exchanged glances. 'All right, Percy,' Pepe said, 'get to it.'

The whole process took less than five minutes. Paras, and then Sufi, marched to the voting desk, scribbled on the voting slips and spoke something to the camera about why they voted the way they did. In her turn, Sulochana wrote the name she had chosen, but only shook her head at the camera.

Pepe milked the suspense as long as he could for what it was worth. He counted Paras's vote and then Sufi's. No surprises: one to each. With Sulochana's vote in his hand, he began talking about the finals—what the finalists should be prepare for, and that the finals would be witnessed by a few star guests from Bollywood. 'And so,' Pepe wound up, 'the people who will have the pleasure of meeting Shaufeek Khan and Ashwini Arora are Sulochana and...' A gap of five seconds later, 'Percy. Sufi, I am afraid your *Real Deal* journey ends here.'

Pepe had landed the knockout punch at so unexpected a moment that it took both Sufi and Paras a few seconds for the conclusion to register. Sulochana could not bear to look at Sufi's face or meet his glance, but at the same time could not tear her gaze away from him. While Paras was leaping ecstatically, and punching the air in triumph, Sufi said, in a steady voice, 'So Mohinder was right. I have nothing to say,

Sulo, you made your choice. What could have been, but now won't be. All the best to both of you.'

After shaking hands with Paras, Sulochana and Pepe, and refusing to grant her an extra moment to exchange significant glances or conversation, he left in a waiting car that would take him away from the venue, without turning back for one last look. Overwhelmed by sadness, she wanted to scream at Pepe that she had written the wrong name on the voting slip. Could she change it; could she take her decision back?

That was the last she had seen of him, and most likely, would also be the last she ever saw or heard from him. And Paras said that she had had no choice but to vote for him! He had no clue how close he had come to being the one going back in that car. Why indeed did she choose him, if not for the feelings of loyalty and gratitude and the inevitable guilt that would haunt her had she chosen Sufi?

Sufi's reaction had told her how genuine his feelings for her were. The shock on his face at the moment of realization in the vote-out was because he understood then that she had chosen Paras over him, and not because he was out of *The Real Deal*. The sight of Paras now, before her, on the bed, only reinforced the contrast he drew with Sufi in her mind. What could she do to stop the utterly useless but persistent question—'What if?'—from racking her? But she also knew that the same question would have arisen even if she had chosen the other way round.

'Well, all right,' Paras spoke up after a sigh, breaking the long silence, 'you did not have to vote him out. Let's forget that now. The important thing to focus on now is that it's you and me. We can't change that. So we decide, what next?'

'What next?' Sulochana repeated, dully.

'Now it's between you and me. Either you win, or I win. One of us has to lose to the other. This is different, right? Now we will be against each other. Do you understand that?'

'Yes, I suppose so,' Sulochana said, forcing her mind away from Sufi to grasp what Paras was babbling about. 'Against each other. That sounds so odd.'

'Exactly!' Paras said, immediately. 'It doesn't feel right to me either. So we need to decide who wins tomorrow.'

'What do you mean, we decide? How can we decide that?'

Paras sighed deeper. 'Look Sulo, actually it doesn't really matter to me whether I win or you win. It's all the same to me.'

'Then why worry who wins tomorrow?'

'That's not what I meant. Shouldn't we discuss our strategy?'

'What for, Paras? What's the point?'

'What's wrong with you, Sulo? Why are you so irritable and difficult today? Okay, you tell me from your point of view who should win tomorrow.'

Sulochana responded to Paras's irritating sighs with one of her own. 'It's the same to me too, Paras, whoever wins. I would rather you win, so that you stop eating my head!'

'Really, you mean that? That I should win?'

'Hold on! Don't take everything I say seriously. If you love me so much, why don't you sacrifice and make me win?'

'Sacrifice? Sure. Of course I can,' Paras said, looking at her curiously. 'But you would also do the same for me given a chance, right?'

'Haven't I shown that already?'

'But that was sacrificing Sufi, not yourself.'

She could slap him. 'What do you want from me, Paras?'

He took a deep breath and said, 'See Sulo, you are already famous. It does not matter whether you win or lose. But if I lose, no one will remember me later.'

'Nonsense.'

'No, really. I bet you will get offers after the show, regardless of whether you win or lose tomorrow.' She could see he was convinced by his own argument. 'Other reality shows or even film offers. People will remember me only if I win tomorrow. How many remember which guy lost the finals last year? But Komal, though she went out much before the finals, is already a VJ on YTV. People don't forget pretty girls.'

'So are you asking me to lose to you deliberately tomorrow?' She knew the answer to her question before she asked it. Apparently, in Paras's mind, she would never be able to pay off her debt; no matter what she did, he would not be propitiated.

'I don't know, Paras,' she continued, 'I didn't come here to lose, at least, not on purpose. You are the one who always motivated me to never give up.'

'But that's different. We love each other. We will always be together even after the show.'

Sulochana paused for a few seconds before saying quietly, 'If it were Sufi in your place, I know he would not have hesitated in giving up his place for me.'

'Oh, really? Too bad you didn't choose him then.'

'Yes, too bad.'

'Fine. He did everything for you in Bisalpur. He was the one who got you here.'

'Oh, all right, keep reminding me that until I die. You gave my interview and GD, didn't you?'

'So you don't remember anything I have done for you?'

'I have not forgotten, Paras. That's why you are still here.' What more did she need to do to make him let go of his claim on her?

The sound of his heavy breathing was audible to her, as though he had just run up a few flights of stairs. 'And if I do let you win, then?' he asked.

'You don't get it. I don't want you to let me win. Let's just not decide—oh, all right, you win,' Sulochana broke off abruptly, tiring of the conversation. 'It doesn't matter to me anymore.'

'Are you sure?' he asked, looking at her closely.

'Do you want me to put it on a stamp paper? Just leave me alone, Paras. I am tired.'

'But, Sulo, I...' he trailed off, probably deciding that any further attempt to extract a promise from her would backfire. A few silent seconds later, Paras got off the bed. 'All right, Sulo. See you tomorrow.' At the door, he turned and said, 'I love you, Sulo, you know. I am still the old Paras of Bisalpur.'

Sulochana tried to keep her mind off Paras and Sufi for the rest of the day, but it was hard, given that she was not allowed to have any other diversion like TV or magazines. She tried to imagine and prepare for the final task but as she had no idea what the task would be, the effort was futile. Finally, in the evening, Pepe summoned her and Paras as well, as she discovered when she reached Pepe's room.

'Sulochana,' Pepe began without any ado, 'the only reason I am giving you this choice is because you know bike riding.

Are you okay with having a bike task in the final? You have the option of saying "no" now. I don't want to make this a last-minute surprise for you.'

'I would love a bike task, Pepe,' Sulochana said without a moment's hesitation. Pepe and the YTV team must have decided that mind games and treasure hunts would not pull in the TRPs, especially for the finals. They wanted guts and glory; what better way than to make use of her biking skills?

'But it is not fair,' Paras said. 'Everyone will support her because she's a girl but still doing a guy task. How will I look competing against her on a bike? You should ask my preference too.'

'I can beat you fair and square on the bike, Paras, you know that,' Sulochana said.

'She's right,' Pepe said. 'I have seen her practise on the bike off the camera. That's real bike love. You, Percy,' Pepe said, turning edgy, 'the reason I called you is that I don't want only Sulochana to have the advantage of knowing the nature of the task tomorrow. Because I am fair. But you guys, please stop talking about fairness. It makes me sick. Thank your stars, and me, that you are still here.'

A milestone revealed they were close to Faridabad. In a win-win understanding with YTV, Shaufeek Khan and Ashwini Arora agreed to bestow their presence on *The Real Deal* in order to promote their forthcoming movie, while lending much needed glamour to the show. They appeared only an hour late, and going by their swagger-filled entry, bereft of any hint of apology, Paras assumed this was considered quite punctual by the stars' standards.

A crowd had been collected to witness the finals without much trouble—another benefit of having Bollywood stars around. While waiting for the actors to arrive, *The Real Deal* crew explained and demonstrated to the crowd when and how to cheer and roar and get to their feet.

Shaufeek Khan's secretary made it clear that they would have to start the proceedings as quickly as possible because they had to be back in Delhi that evening. Soon, Pepe was introducing Sulochana and Paras to the stars. Paras pinched himself to believe that he was actually shaking hands and talking with a superstar, a man whose name everyone in the country knew. Shaufeek was caked in layers of make-up, while Ashwini looked comparatively natural. Sulochana, too, appeared as stunned as he was, when Ashwini wished her all the best for the final.

Pepe, who was showing an embarrassing degree of obsequiousness to the stars, now turned to Sulochana and him. 'Okay guys, this is your final test. This task will test your bike-riding skills, as this show is all about biking and adventure. Sulochana is a great rider, so with her permission we are going ahead with this, or normally we would not devise this kind of contest between a guy and a girl. Do you want to change your mind, Sulochana?'

'No way, Pepe. Once I am on my bike, it will be bike versus bike, not guy versus girl.'

'Bravo!' Ashwini cheered. On cue, the crowd roared its approval.

'What we have here,' Pepe continued, 'is an obstacle course. You ride your bikes, but on the way you have to deal with pits and bumps and narrow passages. There are ten flags of each colour, red and blue, planted at different spots. Whoever picks up all of his or her flags and reaches the finishing line first is our final *Real Deal* champion. You have to pick up the flags from your bike. You cannot get off it. Understand?'

'Yes, sir.' The 'course' was a gravel track running around the oval-shaped ground, or more precisely, in the shape of the letter Q, with the tail of the Q leading towards two closed gates.

The audience was seated in rows of plastic chairs along the lengths of the track, while many others stood beyond the last row to create an impression of a packed stadium.

'Sulochana, which flags do you want? Blue or red?'

'Red.' Of course.

'Fine. Percy, you pick only the blue flags, and Sulochana, you pick only the red ones. Okay with that, Percy?'

'Yes, sir.'

'Are you both ready?'

'Yes, sir.'

'Are you ready?' Pepe asked, now directing his question at the crowd and roaring into his mike.

Again, on cue, the crowd leapt to its feet and roared back.

'All right. Put on your safety gear—helmet, elbow and knee guards. When I say "start", run to your bikes and start. Shake hands like good competitors and begin.'

Her hand felt limp in his. Before putting on his helmet, Paras tried to hold her gaze, but she looked away the instant his glance met hers. 'All the best,' he whispered, but her only acknowledgement was a terse nod.

On his own, Pepe would have liked to drag on this part for at least a few minutes more, but he was clearly under directions to rush it through.

'Hold on. One more thing. To reach the finishing line, after you have collected all your flags, you have go through those gates you see there at the end—again, one red and one blue. One of them is a false gate; it won't let you through. You have to choose the right one and go through that on your bike and then reach the finishing line. Clear? Good, now go. Start!'

Sulochana and Paras set off at a run to the end where their bikes stood ready, with the helmets on the handlebars. Sulochana was off first, while Paras's helmet slipped from his hands in his haste, and he had to dismount and retrieve it as it rolled away. Within a minute, however, he was able to get his nerves under control, blanking out the noise of the crowd and focusing on what he had to do, rather than worry about what Sulochana was up to. He had to win. He could never live it down, losing to a girl on a bike task, though he knew how adept Sulochana had become in handling bikes. But he had no reason to lose. She had promised, hadn't she, that he would win?

The obstacles in the course were well thought out. The pit they had to cross was deep and wide enough for the bikes to go into it, but not too deep to prevent their coming out. The log blocking their path was large enough to make them slow down before going gingerly over it, but again not too large to fully stall them. Two tables standing in the way had a gap wide enough to let only one of them go at a time. Sulochana was marginally ahead of him, so he had to let her go first, though he did try to block her progress for a few seconds before judging that the stalemate would get him nowhere.

In every case, simply skirting the obstacles was not an option, as their progress was hemmed in by bamboo poles tied end to end to mark the boundaries of the track. Some of the flags were placed in easily visible spots. Though prominently visible, sticking out of the bamboo poles on the sides, both of them overlooked the flags in their haste to get ahead. Paras screeched to a halt only when he noticed Sulochana do the same, and make a U-turn to recover her flag. He saw his own blue flag fluttering further behind, and that lapse let Sulochana back into the lead again.

But those flags were the easy pickings, the low-hanging fruits. The others were concealed better, either being difficult to spot, or difficult to reach from the bike. A stretch of red and blue sheets camouflaged some flags; some were stuck to the edge of a table, almost impossible to reach without dismounting from the bike; some fluttering shapes that looked like flags from a distance turned out to be decoys.

What if he let her win instead? If, on the biggest stage of his life, he stepped aside for her to take the limelight, she would be beholden to him for the rest of her life. She would be his forever.

Sulochana collected four flags after completing one circuit of the course, while Paras completed his a few seconds later, holding five blue flags. A brief pause later, they set off again, in pursuit of the ones they had missed in the first try. He found he was closing the gap on her. Was she slowing down a bit deliberately so that he didn't fall too far behind?

Two circuits later, they were still going neck and neck, with nine flags each. If Sulochana was indeed conniving with him to make him win, she was doing a good job of not overplaying her hand. Whoever discovered his or her next flag first was almost bound to win.

Ten seconds later, Paras leapt in joy on spying the corner of his last flag waving from behind a table leg. Almost immediately, as though she was simply waiting all along for him to find his flag first, Sulochana squealed in delight as she extricated her last flag sticking out under one of the barrier logs. She was taking the 'fight' to the wire. Surely no one would have doubted the genuineness of her effort had she 'discovered' her flag a few more seconds later, giving him enough time to reach the finish line first.

At this point, the track leading to the exit gates was between them. So when both Sulochana and Paras thundered towards the exit, they were converging from different directions. In the split second that Paras looked up towards the gates, he realized the blue gate was the false one. It just stood affixed at the sides to its wooden frame, while the red was hinged to one side. Clearly that was the only one of the two that looked capable of swinging open.

He certainly did not have the time to judge that if he chose the blue gate, he would lose the final but win the only girl he had loved forever. And that with his sacrifice, not only would he prove his true worth to her but also show his parents, Bisalpur and the whole world, what the real Percy, Paras or Paras Nath Sharma was made of. He would show them all what the real deal was, in spite of all appearances and the negative impressions he must have evoked so far—that the only things in life that had lasting value were truth and love. He would surprise them all, wouldn't he, if he went for the blue gate, knowing very well that it was the door to nowhere? Sulochana, by default, would then reach the red gate and the triumph that lay beyond it. While, if he touched the red one first, he would grasp only ephemeral joy but lose what was noble and good and eternal. If that was too much of an abstraction to be convincing, in more concrete terms, he would lose Sulochana forever, and most likely to Sufi.

Paras had instinctively known all along, without his being aware, that he was destined to face this dilemma. At the last instant, beyond which it would not matter what he decided, he burst out towards the doorway he wanted.

As he hurtled onto the exit track, eyes intent on the red gate, he did not notice Sulochana squeezing out the last throb of power from her bike, leaping out on a collision course with him. He saw her at the very last moment when she was almost upon him. His bike shook and shied like a skittish horse before righting itself. Within those lost couple of seconds, she was at the red gate, trying to nudge it open with her front wheel. He had almost caught up with her when on her second attempt, she pushed the gate open and with a final spurt of the accelerator, jumped ahead and crossed the finishing line. The crowd roared. It did not need a cue this time.

'I have lived my dream,' Sulochana said. That was the first and only line that struck her, and stayed with her. She said it first to herself when she crossed the finishing line and realized that Paras was one bike-length behind her. She told Pepe when Pepe hugged her and held her arm aloft as if he was a boxing referee announcing the winner of the bout. She repeated it when Shaufeek Khan handed over *The Real Deal* champion trophy to her, asked her how she felt and invited her to the premiere of his new movie launching two weeks later. And she would say it over and again to the several interviewers and cameras that she would face over the next few days and weeks, once the final episode had been telecast. By then, of course, she would add a great many more good lines to say.

The only one who reacted to this line negatively was Paras. He could not find a moment to talk to her while she basked in the glory of her triumph, after the presentation of the trophy, followed by an over-the-top ceremony of crowning her as *The Real Deal* Champion, Season 5, on a gaudy throne. But eventually, descending from her throne, she noticed him some distance away, looking wistfully at the seat she had just vacated.

'Well played, Sulo, well played!' he remarked, walking up to her and clapping his hands sardonically. 'To betray the very person who brought you here...that requires guts.'

'Oh, Paras, I am sure you never betrayed anyone here. But what does betrayal and loyalty and friendship really mean on this show?'

As Paras's face fell on hearing his own words thrown back at him, she felt sorry for the forlorn figure he was cutting. There was no need for this bitterness. She had won, he had lost—he couldn't be feeling worse.

'Look, Paras, it doesn't matter now.'

'It doesn't matter now.'

Both spoke at the same time, and looked at each other wryly for saying the same thing. At an earlier time—now seeming an eternity ago—they would have considered themselves soulmates for echoing each other's thoughts.

Yes, it did not matter now because what was done was done. You could not reverse the events of the last hour, try again and reach a different ending. For this was an ending, equally obvious to both. But he deserved an explanation, if nothing more.

'I...I didn't come here to lose, Paras, I told you. Not on purpose for sure.'

Paras said nothing.

'I truly wanted to win for my father. That wasn't just a line I said for the camera. I really meant it. But you never believed that, did you?'

'So it wasn't your revenge for sending Sufi out?' he asked, not quite hiding a smirk.

'No!' Maybe at a subconscious level, it was. She was not sure. 'I realized I didn't owe you anything more. That's why I did what I did. After I sent Sufi out, we were clear. We were done.'

'Is that how you saw us? As an obligation?' His tone was so incredulous that she almost believed her revelation came as a surprise to him.

A reporter, with a cameraman in tow, was approaching them. Paras saw them and said, 'Your new life is beginning. Congrats, Sulo. I suppose you deserved to win. When did you realize that the blue gate was fake?'

She looked puzzled. 'No, I just went for the red one. You know I like red.'

Paras stared at her for a second and then burst out laughing. 'Of course. Because you like red.'

'Miss Sulochana?' the reporter asked. 'I am from *The Delhi Times*. Can we have an interview now?

'Maybe we will meet again in Bisalpur, Sulo, if you ever come back,' Paras said, withdrawing. 'All the best.'

Sulochana nodded. He would manage. He would get out of Bisalpur too, somehow or the other, sooner or later. She turned to the reporter. 'Right now?'

'Yes, ma'am.'

She hesitated for a moment. She followed Paras with her gaze, as he receded rapidly from her, until he became an indistinctive figure in the dispersing crowd.

'Shoot. What are your questions?'

'What is your immediate reaction on winning the title? What are your plans for the future?'

'The feeling is amazing,' Sulochana began. 'I feel I have lived my dream. And my father's.'

'Turn on the camera, you fool!' the reporter yelled at his cameraman.

'We can go over the questions again,' Sulochana suggested, helpfully. 'Make sure you record it this time.'

'Just a second,' the cameraman said. 'Right. Ready now.'

'I have lived my dream. And my father's,' Sulochana said. She could repeat the lines over and over, and never tire of it.

ACKNOWLEDGEMENTS

I am grateful to:

Ahmed Faiyaz and Kanishka Gupta, for believing in this novel.

Meghna Singhee and Amrita Mukerji, whose editing and suggestions have helped make the book much better than it was originally.

Sheena Dabholkar, for her invaluable inputs about the making of a TV reality show.

Most of all, my wife Smita, my son Palash, my parents, my sister Shweta and my nephew Prajjwal, for providing me a happy and supportive family environment to work in.